NORFOLK LIBRARY
AND INFORMATION SERVICE

D1427919

SHERLOCK HOLMES
AND THE GIANT'S HAND

Three of the great detective's most singular cases, mentioned tantalisingly briefly in the original narratives, are now presented here in full. The curious disappearance of Mr Stanislaus Addleton leads Holmes and Watson ultimately to the mysterious 'Giant's Hand'. What peculiar brand of madness drives Colonel Warburton to repeatedly attack an amiable village vicar? Then there is the murderous tragedy of the Abernetty family, the solving of which hinges on the depth to which the parsley had sunk into the butter on a hot day . . .

MATTHEW BOOTH

SHERLOCK HOLMES AND THE GIANT'S HAND

Complete and Unabridged

LINFORD
Leicester

First published in Great Britain by
Baker Street Studios Limited
Cambridge

First Linford Edition
published 2008
by arrangement with
Baker Street Studios Limited
Cambridge

British Library CIP Data

Booth, Matthew
Sherlock Holmes and the giant's hand
and other stories.—Large print ed.—
Linford mystery library
1. Holmes, Sherlock (Fictitious character)—
Fiction 2. Watson, John H. (Fictitious character)
—Fiction 3. Detective and mystery stories
4. Large type books
I. Title
823.9'2 [F]

ISBN 978–1–84782–142–3

Published by
F. A. Thorpe (Publishing)
Anstey, Leicestershire

Set by Words & Graphics Ltd.
Anstey, Leicestershire
Printed and bound in Great Britain by
T. J. International Ltd., Padstow, Cornwall

This book is printed on acid-free paper

Contents

The Adventure of the Giant's Hand

When I glance over my notes of our work for the year 1894, I find it very difficult to select those affairs which are most interesting in themselves and at the same time illustrate those amazing faculties by which Mr Sherlock Holmes was distinguished. Several of these I have already recorded: those members of the public who have taken some interest in this series of memoirs will recall that the year '94 presented us with the affair of the Norwood Builder and the punishment of Mr Jonas Oldacre, as well as the tragic death at Yoxley Old Place. There were many other cases brought before my friend, however, and one particular case was so singular in its nature and presented so clearly an example of my companion's gifts that these accounts would be

1

incomplete without some report of it. I refer to the singular disappearance of Mr Stanislaus Addleton and the contents of the ancient British barrow.

My notes tell me that it was a cold brisk morning in autumn and Holmes and I were seated at the breakfast table, enjoying a plate of rashers and eggs when the landlady brought in the morning post. When she had left us, Sherlock Holmes tore open envelope after envelope, tossing their contents to the floor with a snort of contempt. Presently however he fell silent, and read and re-read one particular letter. For some time I watched him, his square chin resting upon his hand and his grey austere eyes darting over the words before him. Finally, he glanced at me and handed me the correspondence, which had given him this puzzling quarter of an hour. The note was written on a sheet of foolscap and was in a hand that was familiar to me. It was from Inspector Hopkins and ran as follows:

Malvere Towers
Fairdale
Cornwall

My dear Mr Holmes,
   I should be very glad of your immediate assistance in what promises to be a most remarkable case and something quite in your line. If it is convenient to you, I shall call upon you this morning and lay the full facts before you. There is, as far as I can tell, no clue, and I should very much value your advice.

Yours,
STANLEY HOPKINS

Stanley Hopkins was a police inspector for whose future Holmes had high hopes. In turn, Hopkins professed the admiration and respect of a pupil for the methods of the famous amateur. On each occasion, Hopkins's summons had proved entirely justified, and every one of his cases has, I think, found its way into this collection. It was therefore with a mixture of eagerness and impatience that we waited for

Hopkins's hand upon our bell. We were not kept waiting too long, however, and in a short time, we heard Hopkins's step on the stair and the tall alert young man was standing in the doorway.

Holmes ushered him in and seated him in the vacant chair upon which a newcomer must sit. For some moments, Hopkins's keen eyes darted around the room, as though he were possessed by a great anxiety. His brows were furrowed and his shoulders weighed down with a heavy dejection. Finally, however, he turned his gaze onto Sherlock Holmes with a look of absolute despair.

'I feel I must apologize for my haste in communicating with you,' said he, 'but there is no time to be lost. I am at my wits' end.'

Holmes sank into his armchair and filled his pipe from the Persian slipper. 'Your note was scarce as to details.'

'My only thought was to get here as soon as possible, Mr Holmes. I have been at Malvere Towers since yesterday and I have made no progress at all.'

'State your case,' said Holmes in his

brisk, business-like tones.

'It is difficult to know where to begin,' said Hopkins, drawing his official notebook from his inside pocket. 'Have you heard of the name Stanislaus Addleton?'

'Make a long arm, Watson,' said Holmes, 'and see what our index has to say.'

I flicked through the volume he indicated and read aloud the following entry:

ADDLETON, STANISLAUS: Born 1840. Widowed. One son, Raymond; one daughter, Violet. Resides at Malvere Towers, Fairdale, Cornwall. Historian, philosopher; specialized subject being Ancient Greece and Rome. Author of 'Romulus & Remus: a Study in Fraternal Alliance'; 'An Investigation into the Life of Alexander the Great'; 'The Law and Order of Draco'. Also the author of various articles upon the Persian and Trojan Wars, and the discovery of Rome. Educated Cambridge, 1859–1862. M.A., Ph.D., etc. etc.

'A man of singular accomplishments,' observed Holmes. 'What is it about Mr Stanislaus Addleton which need necessarily concern us, Hopkins?'

The inspector regarded us with his keen, alert eyes and replied in a soft voice: 'Mr Stanislaus Addleton has vanished without trace.'

I confess that a thrill passed through my heart at Hopkins's words, but my companion showed no indication of any excitement upon his part. He remained motionless in his armchair and smiled kindly at the official policeman.

'My good Hopkins,' said he, 'as long as a man stands upon two legs, so long must there be some physical trace of his existence.'

'I assure you, sir, that there is no trace of Mr Addleton.'

'Meaning you have found none. Come, come, Hopkins, this is not your usual self.' Holmes rose and poured some coffee, which he handed to our visitor. He settled back in his armchair, closed his eyes and placed his fingertips together. 'Give us a full account of the affair, and pray, be precise as to details.'

'I've got my facts pretty clear,' said Stanley Hopkins. 'All I want to know now is what they all mean. As far as I can make out, the story is this: Stanislaus Addleton is a widower, who lost his wife seven years ago to consumption. He took up residence at Malvere Towers shortly after the tragedy, and his daughter Violet joined him there, having recently left a boarding establishment in Edinburgh. The house itself is a marvel. I doubt whether in all England there is a more secluded and self-contained house. It stands in its own grounds, surrounded by a high brick wall, and so near the coast is it that the sea can be heard lashing the rocks below, even at the height of activity in the house.

'I turn now to the particular events which have brought me here today. Monday was Miss Addleton's birthday, and her father held a small celebration for her. Present were Mr Addleton and his daughter; his son, Raymond; and Mr Addleton's personal medical adviser and friend, Dr Eustace Tewson. It seems that

Mr Addleton is something of a recluse, who shuns the company of his fellow man, which may explain the small gathering around the table. Dinner was served by Muir, the butler, and Mary Dobson, the maid, at half past seven precisely. They all remember hearing the large clock in the hallway chime. At ten o'clock, once the gifts had been received, both Violet and Raymond retired to bed. Dr Tewson retired an hour later, and the owner of the house moved to his study. Both the doctor and Muir observed him do so.

'Half an hour later, Muir was about his rounds, ensuring that the windows and doors were all fastened, when he saw Mr Addleton putting on his topcoat. It was not his custom to leave the house after dark, and his behaviour at once alerted Muir to some problem. Mr Addleton told the butler not to wait for him, and to bolt the door. Thus, entry could only be obtained by the use of a key, and only Mr Addleton and his son had such a key. Supposing that he intended to return, Mr Addleton must have had his key about his person. The lack of any luggage indicated that he did indeed intend to return. I was fairly certain upon that point.

'Mr Addleton was, by habit, the first to rise for breakfast. However, the following morning, the household were surprised to find no sign of their host. A search of the house proved fruitless, and his bed had not been slept in. His possessions, however, were all to be found in his bedroom. When he had not returned by the afternoon, the local police were informed, but they turned up nothing. Thus, I was sent for and upon my arrival threw myself into a thorough investigation.'

Stanley Hopkins paused in his singular narrative and gulped at the coffee that Holmes had poured out for him. My friend did not move during the interval, but remained motionless, with his eyes tightly closed.

'The sum of my findings,' continued Hopkins, 'is small indeed. Having established the facts that I have just outlined to you, I made a thorough examination of the study, where Mr Addleton had last been seen. My eye was caught by a large safe in the corner of the room. It was a magnificent example of its kind, and according to Mr Raymond Addleton it contained his father's business papers. The nature of these papers is unknown to him, however. The door of the safe was open, and when I looked inside, I found . . . ' He faltered for a moment and caught his breath. 'Mr Holmes, the safe was empty!'

'Remarkable,' said Holmes.

'And yet no one knew the combination except Mr Addleton himself. But what has become of the papers? Two other points struck me about the room. The first was a gold watch, which was lying upon the table. It had stopped due to its not being wound that night, and the time it said was midnight. The proximity of this hour to that when Mr Addleton left the house alerted me to the importance of the watch, but what it signified I could not tell. The final point was to be found on the blotter on the centre of the desk. There, in handwriting which I have established as being Mr Addleton's own, was the following message.'

The inspector handed us a small piece of paper. Written across it, in Hopkins's own hand, were the words:

'tumuli: Barclay instalment'

'The original was written exactly as I have reproduced it. It was scrawled across the blotter, presumably to avoid its being lost or mislaid.

'Well, sir, those are the main facts of the case, and I am bound to say that even with all these threads in my hands, I am unable to make sense of the matter. I know your methods, Mr Sherlock Holmes, and I tried to apply them, but I am no further now than before I arrived at Malvere Towers. I communicated with you at once and came around as soon as I could to put the matter in your hands.'

Sherlock Holmes had been examining the piece of paper that Hopkins had handed to him. For some time we sat in silence, as Holmes's keen grey eyes darted over the words in front of him. Finally, he handed the enigmatic message back to the inspector and re-filled his pipe.

'What do you make of this message?' he asked.

'I can make nothing of it.'

'There does not seem to be one point which strikes you as vital?'

'The latter half of the message obviously points to some payment owed by someone called Barclay.'

'A wager no doubt,' I said.

'No doubt,' muttered Holmes, although I could see he was far from satisfied. 'How about the watch?'

'It has been identified as Mr Addleton's. His son is certain of the fact.'

'There is no explanation for its being left behind?'

'None.'

'You have formed none yourself?' asked Holmes, his eyes suddenly regaining their fire, as they so often did when the fit was upon him.

Hopkins looked at his notes with a severe look of disappointment. 'I can find nothing to reconcile the facts.'

'It is certainly an interesting case,' said

Holmes. 'I suppose I shall have to come and have a look at it.'

Stanley Hopkins gave a cry of joy, and wrung Holmes's hand in gratitude.

'Thank you, sir, thank you indeed. It would certainly be a weight off my mind.'

'Watson, if you can spare the time, I should be very glad of your company.'

'By all means.'

'Excellent!' Holmes turned to Stanley Hopkins with a kindly smile. 'If you will call a four wheeler, we shall be ready to start for Malvere Towers in a quarter of an hour.'

★ ★ ★

The journey to Cornwall was subdued, and we travelled in silence. Sherlock Holmes sat in the corner of the carriage, his sharp face framed in his ear-flapped travelling cap and his knitted brows and abstracted eyes betraying the deep thought with which he employed his mind. Hopkins too sat in silence, checking through his notes lest there be any point of importance which he had failed to mention. For myself, I settled back in the cushions, idly watching the dun-coloured houses of the capital disappear into the manufactured clouds of the train's chimney. In a very few hours, the greys had become green and the brown earth had become ruddy, as the lush grasses and luxuriant vegetation spoke of a richer, if damper, climate.

From the small station at Fairdale, we hired a dogcart to take us to Malvere Towers. As on the train, Holmes sat buried in the deepest thought, with his arms folded and his cap pulled over his eyes. Stanley Hopkins had put away his notebook and endeavoured to gain some information from my companion. So intense was the expression on Holmes's face, however, that it seemed a futile task.

At last we stopped, and alighted at a pair of large iron gates. Before us stood a very large stone building, surrounded, as Hopkins had said, by a high brick wall. The building was three storeys high and at either end was a large, cylindrical tower, which gave the impression of a medieval fortress. As we walked down the gravel pathway that led to the house, we could see a stone archway which framed the oak-panelled door of the entrance. Latticed windows peered out from behind excessive ivy and onto the extensive and somewhat exemplary gardens.

Hopkins rapped on the door and we waited for a reply. Holmes was glancing about him and I knew him well enough to realize that the seemingly cursory glance had taken in every detail that was visible to him. We were, as the inspector had said, so near the coast that the sea could be heard clearly from the distance. The waves crashed against the rocks with a ferocity that seemed to add to the disturbing mystery that hung over the house and I confess that the sound, which usually thrills and cheers me, filled my soul with a certain horror.

The heavy wooden door opened and we were greeted by a small, pugnacious man whose stiff and military bearing, and immaculate frock coat, suggested his position of servitude. This, no doubt, was

Muir the butler. Standing to one side, he allowed us to enter, having been introduced by Hopkins. We entered the hallway and were approached by a young man of thirty or so. He was very dark, with clear and expressive eyes and a black, waxed moustache, which suited his thin face well enough to display his good looks. On his arm was a girl of no more than three and twenty, with a well-formed and intelligent face, and that very dark hair which was so prominent in the man. Her cheeks, however, were very pale and her eyes were heavy, indicating that she had not slept well. At the sight of Hopkins, they both ran forward eagerly.

'Have you any news, inspector?' asked the man.

'Is there any clue?' added the girl.

'No, Mr Addleton; but Mr Holmes has come down from London to help us.'

'Mr Holmes of Baker Street?' exclaimed the young man.

My friend bowed. Mr Addleton shook his hand warmly, and at the mention of Holmes's name, the colour seemed to return to his sister's cheeks.

'My name is Raymond Addleton, and this is my sister, Violet. We hope you might be able to throw some light on these circumstances which have vexed us.'

'You may rely upon me doing all that I can,' replied Holmes. 'There are one or two points upon which I should like some clarification. The watch found in the study — I understand it belonged to your father.'

'Yes. It belonged to my grandfather originally and was bequeathed to my father when the old man died.'

'Can you offer any explanation for its being left behind?'

'None. My father was fond of it, and seldom so careless.'

'The point may be a minor one,' murmured Sherlock Holmes. 'May we turn to the safe. It had been emptied, is that not so?'

'That is correct.'

'You had seen inside the safe, I believe, Mr Addleton?'

'Once. It was full of papers tied up with red silk.'

'Who would have a combination to the safe?'

Mr Raymond Addleton paused for a moment and his brows creased in thought. 'No one as far as I am aware, Mr Holmes.'

'You did not know it yourself?'

'No.'

'Nor you, Miss Addleton?'

The girl turned her dark, swollen eyes upon my companion. 'No, sir,' said she with some delicacy.

'Most interesting,' said Holmes, as much to himself as to us. 'How then do you explain the contents being removed?'

'It is possible my father had taken them out and taken them with him,' said Raymond Addleton.

'Of course. I had not thought of that.'

There was something in Holmes's manner and his tone, which suggested to me that he was not entirely satisfied with the explanation offered by Raymond Addleton. With a smile and a bow, he thanked them for their time and expressed his desire to see the study where Mr Stanislaus Addleton had last been seen.

This was a lofty chamber, lined with innumerable volumes, the titles of which were as obscure as their subjects. A large set of French windows was set into the far wall, and a writing bureau stood to the side of them. Papers, notes and jottings were scattered across it and a pile of addressed envelopes was stacked in the centre. A large writing desk, leather topped and ornately varnished, stood in the centre of the room; a large white blotter was in the middle, filled with ink blemishes and scribbles which are so often to be found on such items. Behind the desk was a red, velvet armchair, which concealed the large safe of which Hopkins had spoken. The door was open and, as the inspector had said, it was empty.

Holmes surveyed the room, his keen eyes darting from one item to the next with his customary glance. The French windows, the desk, the bureau and the fireplace were in turn subjected to the most careful examination. Some items he considered with his naked eye;

others he scrutinized under his magnifying lens. The fireplace, for the moment, held his utmost attention, and he kneeled by the grate and thrust his fingers into the ashes. So engrossed was he in his occupation that he appeared to have forgotten our presence.

'Am I to understand,' said he at last, 'that the papers which were in the safe were bound by red silk?'

'That is correct, Mr Holmes,' returned Hopkins, and Mr Raymond Addleton concurred.

'There is, then, no mystery as to what has happened to the papers,' remarked Sherlock Holmes carelessly.

He rose and held up a small piece of red silk, blackened at either end by the flames of the previous night's fire. Having stared at it through his lens for some moments, Holmes handed the silk to Hopkins with a smile.

'This is a dog-grate, and whoever threw the papers into the fire over-pitched his aim. But you have been sloppy, Hopkins,' said he. 'A mere glance at the fireplace would have told you all you needed to know.'

'The papers have been burned,' said the inspector with some dejection.

'But why should Mr Addleton burn his own papers?' I asked. 'There was only he with access to them.'

Sherlock Holmes had seated himself at the writing desk and was looking at the blotter before him. 'That is only one of the mysteries which we have to solve. What do you make of this, Watson?'

I moved over to the desk and peered over his shoulder. I saw for myself the enigmatic message, which had so puzzled Hopkins:

'tumuli: Barclay instalment'

'I can make nothing of it,' I confessed.

' 'Barclay instalment'. Does that suggest nothing to your mind?'

'I must agree with Hopkins. It seems to refer to a wager of some kind.'

Holmes shook his head like a man who is far from satisfied. 'There is surely something more to it than that.'

He rose, and walked over to the writing

bureau. From there, he looked over his shoulder at Mr Raymond Addleton and his sister and addressed them directly. 'Can you offer any explanation as to why your father should burn his own papers?'

'None,' replied Miss Addleton.

'Mr Raymond?'

'I cannot think. I have only caught a brief glimpse of them in the past, but can think of no reason for him to destroy them.'

'Have you heard of the name Jeremiah Dawson?'

'Never.'

'Nor Annabella Wright?'

'No, Mr Holmes, but — '

Holmes held up his hand to silence the young man, and picked up from the bureau the stack of envelopes to which I have alluded. He thumbed through them and handed them to Mr Raymond and his sister. Both of them looked at the names in puzzlement.

'I have never heard of any of these people,' said the girl.

'Well, well,' said Holmes blandly, 'it is nothing. If I could ask you to excuse us for a moment, we will join you presently.'

Somewhat reluctantly, the young couple took their leave and Hopkins closed the door behind them. Leaning against the door, the young inspector groaned miserably.

'I feel such a fool,' said he. 'I should have observed the remnants of the papers in the fire.'

Holmes was examining in minute detail the golden watch, which lay upon the desk. He stared at the chain and its links before scrutinizing the case. At Hopkins's words, he looked at the grim official.

'Do not torture yourself, my good sir,' said he gently. 'If I read the riddle aright, the importance of the safe's contents has not been entirely lost. But this watch, Hopkins; why did you not tell me of its condition?'

'I do not follow you.'

'You no doubt observed the key hanging from the end of the chain?'

'I did not attach any importance to it.'

'You surprise me!' exclaimed Sherlock Holmes. 'It seems to me to be of the utmost importance. The ring that attaches the key to the first link of the chain is also of some interest. If you examine it through my glass, you will see that the ring is misshapen and bent.'

Hopkins examined the gold watch through the lens. 'Why yes! It is slightly twisted.'

'But how are we to find the lock which matches the key?' I asked.

'There is no great mystery in that, my dear Watson,' said Holmes. 'I shall lay you odds of two to one that the key will unlock the front door. A little experiment is needed I think.'

Grasping the watch in his thin hand, he made his way to the door. Something caught his eye, however, and he paused at a large, varnished bookcase. He ran his finger along the spines of the volumes contained therein, and eventually pulled out a slim volume, which he held aloft.

'This bears the name of our missing historian,' said he. 'One of Mr Addleton's numerous works to be published.'

'Yes,' said Hopkins. 'I believe he has a number of books to his credit.'

Holmes had been flicking through the

pages and to my surprise he gave a cry of satisfaction at one particular page. I looked over his shoulder and saw a large paragraph of writing, the general sense of which I noted as being ancient burial rites. There was, however, nothing so far as I could see which could have so pleased my companion. Holmes, however, laughed in the peculiar, silent fashion which was characteristic of him, and tossed the book over to Hopkins.

'Take this, inspector, and catch up on your history,' said he. 'Now, it is time to put our theory as to this key to the test.' So saying, he marched out of the study with Hopkins and I at his heels. He walked to the front door through which we had entered and pulled it open. He stepped back over the threshold and beckoned me over.

'Would you be so kind as to lock the door, Watson, just as Muir did that night?'

I did so, and Hopkins and I heard Holmes attempt to effect an entry. It was clear that any effort to enter whilst the door was thus locked was impossible. Then, through the heavy wooden door we heard the sound of the key in the lock and a cry of satisfaction from my friend, as the door swung open. Sherlock Holmes stood in the doorway like a magician at the end of an illusion, with a triumphant and self-satisfied smile upon his lips.

'A pretty demonstration,' said he.

'The case grows darker instead of clearer,' I said.

'I agree,' replied Hopkins. 'If Mr Addleton left the house and Muir locked the door after him, why did he not take his own key with him?'

'The case clears every instant, gentlemen,' said Sherlock Holmes. 'I wonder if we might have a word or two with Muir?'

The butler was sent for and he arrived with the promptness for which his position of employment was noted. He bowed as he approached, having lost none of his quiet confidence and reserve which had so impressed me earlier, and waited for one of us to speak. It was Holmes who broke the silence.

'Do you recognize this watch, Muir?'

'It is Mr Addleton's own watch,' replied the butler.

'Was he wearing it last night?'

'He was never without it.'

'When you observed your master putting on his coat last night, did you happen to notice whether Mr Addleton was wearing his watch then?'

'I can't be positive, sir, but I should say he was. He would need it for his key at least.' Muir pointed with a stubby finger at the watch and the key that dangled from the end of the chain. My friend smiled and indicated the twisted ring that held the key in place.

'Can you think of any reason for this ring to be so damaged?' he asked.

'None. Mr Addleton was hardly likely to be so careless. Especially with an heirloom like that.'

'Now then, Muir — and this point is vital — did you lock the door last night as normal?'

'Yes, sir.'

'You are certain?'

Muir stiffened and seemed to sense some criticism in the execution of his duties. His tone of voice betrayed his thoughts. 'Quite certain, sir.'

'Can you throw any light upon the happening of last night?'

The butler shook his head. 'No, sir,' said he. 'I was not aware anything was wrong until after breakfast. I was under the impression that Mr Addleton had returned last night.'

'What made you think so?'

'I heard the door close, sir. Only gently, mind you, but I distinctly heard it. I had not yet retired and was having trouble securing one of the windows in the dining room.'

'What time was this?'

'I cannot be sure, sir, but after midnight I should say.'

'Did you see who it was who closed the door?'

'No, sir. I took it for granted that it was Mr Addleton.'

'Thank you, that is all,' said Holmes. He watched the butler withdraw and placed the watch in his pocket. For a few moments he looked from Hopkins to myself with one of those mischievous twinkles in his eyes which so often implies a dawning light. And yet, I confess that I could not see even the briefest of glimmers.

Hopkins seemed unable to bear my companion's reticence any longer and gripped Holmes by the arm. 'Have you any views, Mr Holmes?'

'There are one or two points which seem to me to be suggestive.'

'But what has become of Mr Stanislaus Addleton?'

'You ought to be able to form some theory to that particular riddle from the watch.'

'The watch?' said I incredulously.

'To be precise,' replied Holmes, 'the twisted link on the chain.'

'That is important?' exclaimed Hopkins.

'Exceedingly so.' And no more would he say on the matter. Instead, he decided he would like to take tea, and strode off in the direction of the drawing room.

In this room, we found Raymond Addleton and his sister, Violet, in conversation with a tall, wiry man with grizzled hair and a large domed forehead. He was dressed well, with a ruby cravat pin and a long cigarette holder completing the picture of an aristocratic dandy. Upon our entrance, they all three looked up at us, and Miss Addleton rushed over to my friend.

'Have you discovered anything new, Mr Holmes?' she implored, her eyes straining themselves upon his face.

'Nothing certain as yet,' answered Holmes. 'But the shadows will no doubt lift.'

'Let us hope you will be able to see something when we have been so blind.'

This new voice belonged to the patrician gentleman with the ruby stud and the cigarette holder. He was introduced as Dr Eustace Tewson, whose name I remembered from Hopkins's narrative at Baker Street. Upon his formal introduction to Sherlock Holmes, the doctor bowed with a reverential smile.

'It is a pleasure to meet the detective who stands alone both in his gifts and his experience. I look forward to seeing your particular talents for myself.'

'Thank you,' said Holmes. 'I perceive that you have recently returned from a visit to Yorkshire, the place of your birth.'

'Yes,' replied Dr Tewson. 'But how did you know that?'

'And how long have you been interested in making pottery?'

Dr Tewson laughed heartily, and turned his dark eyes upon me. 'I see that you have not exaggerated Mr Holmes's abilities, Dr Watson! How on earth did you know all that, sir?'

Holmes waved his hand to brush the compliments aside. 'It is merely a matter of observation. There is a trace of distinctive brown soil on the toe of your right shoe, which indicates that you have been in the country recently. The soil is peculiar to the North of England; hence you have visited that part of the country in the past few weeks. Although your speech betrays your education and position, you are unable to disguise completely the broad vowels of the Yorkshire accent, which shows that particular county as your place of origin. Given that you visited the North recently, it is not too fanciful to suppose that you went back to your roots, as it were.'

'And the pottery?'

'That is even simpler. Under the nail of your left index finger is a small quantity of modelling clay, which suggests that you have spent some time at a potter's wheel. There is no magic or wizardry involved.'

'You have certainly earned your reputation, Mr Holmes,' said Dr Tewson, and he settled back in his chair.

Violet Addleton poured out some tea and handed the cups around to each of us. Holmes took his cup gratefully and sipped his tea in silence for a moment or two. There was an atmosphere in the room, which I found difficult to dispel. It was not an air of anxiety or even of sadness; rather, I fancy, it was of disappointed unease. The people in the room seemed to look at Sherlock Holmes in the expectation of something miraculous, as though his very presence might conjure up the missing man. My friend, however, simply stared out of the window at the extensive lawns that surrounded the house. There was a vase of moss roses on a small table in front of him, and I saw him look at them with a smile upon his lips and a glint of emotion in his eyes. Finally, he turned away from the window, drained his cup and moved to the centre of the room.

'There are one or two questions that I should like to ask,' said he.

Raymond Addleton rose and pulled at his waxed moustache. 'We are all attention,' said he.

'Does anybody in this room know — or have the means of discovering — the combination to the safe in the study?'

There was silence.

'I must have truthful answers to these questions,' said Holmes sternly, but the silence continued. 'Very well. We will pass over that point. Does anybody in this house remember anything that Mr Addleton said last night, which might have indicated his intention to leave?'

'He said nothing to betray such an intention,' said Dr Tewson.

'He didn't say very much all night,' said Violet Addleton. 'I remember asking him if he was unwell, but he replied that he was fine. He said it was my night and that

I should be the centre of everybody's attention.'

I knew Holmes well enough to see in his eyes that the interview was not going as he had wished. His grey eyes were filled with frustration and his thin fingers were restless. Finally, he nodded and moved over to the door.

'One last point: does anybody here recognize the word 'tumuli'?'

Raymond Addleton nodded. 'I have heard father mention the word, but he never explained what it meant.'

'You do not know yourself?'

'No.'

'How often did he mention the word?'

'Only when he was talking about his particular area of expertise.'

'Which was quite often,' added Dr Tewson. 'He was always harping on about some ancient rite or custom.'

'Thank you, that is everything,' said Holmes.

Hopkins moved to Holmes's side and tapped him on the shoulder. 'Well, Mr Holmes? What course do you recommend?'

Holmes pulled his ear-flapped cap onto his head. 'For yourself, Hopkins, I should begin by writing up your reports, and then extending your knowledge with that excellent book which I have recommended to you. As for Watson and myself, a gentle stroll in the grounds would be excellent to work off breakfast.'

The grounds were, as I have stated, extensive, but they were of such a beauty that it was impossible not to be overwhelmed by them. The lawns were neatly trimmed, and the morning dew, which had lain upon them all morning, was at last thawing, so that the moisture lay upon the greenery like divine tears. A brisk breeze whipped our faces as we walked, and in the background there was the sound of the impressive ocean lashing against the coastline. Trees were in abundance, and lines of oaks and beeches stretched far beyond the house into the very depths of the grounds. Small shoots erupted from the soil at our feet, and fully developed flowers were scattered like paintwork across the green canvas. Of course, the beauty of the gardens seemed to be lost on Sherlock Holmes, who put his arm through mine and led me off away from the house, his lips compressed and his brows knitted in concentration.

'What do you make of the business, Watson?' said he, when the house was far behind us.

'I can make nothing of it. Each new fact seems to complicate the issue rather than elucidating it.'

'How so?'

'Well, why should a man burn his own papers? It seems probable that only Mr Addleton could have burned the contents of the safe, since he was the only man with a combination to it. Furthermore,' I continued, 'why should that same man walk out of his own house, leaving his key behind, and fail to return, having made no mention of his intention to disappear?'

'And where is he now?' prompted Holmes, and I seemed to detect in his eyes the glimmer of mischief, which often meant that he had some idea of the truth.

'You have a theory?' I said.

We stopped walking at a small garden

seat, and Holmes sat down and motioned for me to join him. Leaning forward with some eagerness, he sketched out with his forefinger the points to which he alluded on the palm of his hand.

'There are one or two details in this case which have guided me towards the truth,' said he. 'In the first instance, I am not in the least convinced that Mr Stanislaus Addleton burned his own papers. It is my conjecture that someone quite different did so, after Mr Addleton had left the house.'

'But who?' I stammered. 'And how did this person — whoever they may be — gain access to the safe?'

'As to the latter point I have no definite proof, although there is a clear impression in my mind. A more interesting question is *why* this person should burn the papers. The fact that Mr Addleton saw fit to bind the papers together with expensive red silk seems to indicate that he thought they were of some vital importance. Now why should anyone burn such important documents? What did you make of the envelopes which I found on the bureau?'

'Mr Raymond Addleton and his sister knew nothing about them.'

'Precisely, and yet their father must have known these people to be writing to them. Mark that, Watson, and remember it.'

I thought for a moment. 'Might they not be business associates of Mr Addleton?' I suggested.

Holmes seemed unconvinced. 'Were they business partners, why keep their names secret from his children? And the man is a recluse, remember, and so has no close friends. Turn your mind now to the mysterious message found on the blotter.'

' 'tumuli: Barclay instalment',' I quoted, checking through my notebook.

'Precisely. Banish from your mind any preposterous theory Hopkins may have formed about it being a reference to a wager. The idea is unthinkable! Consider the word 'instalment'. Does it not indicate to you a *regular* payment of some description? A continuous payment made

38

over a period of time?'

'It is possible.'

'What then do you make of the message?'

'It suggests nothing to my mind.'

'But it does to my mind, Watson! It suggests something of the very blackest nature! Regular payments are made to a man either regarding or by somebody called Barclay. Various envelopes are found addressed to strangers, of whose existence the man's family is ignorant, but this man shuns the company of his fellow humans. Then the man's important papers are burned, and he himself suddenly and mysteriously disappears. It is not too fanciful to suppose that evil has come upon the man. When you look at the facts in this way, Watson, does still nothing occur to you?'

Suddenly, the clouds lifted in my mind and I had the sense of a vague outline before me. I saw what Holmes was hinting at, and his sharp, intelligent face showed that my thoughts matched his own.

'Blackmail,' I said softly.

'Precise, deliberate, fatal blackmail, my

dear Watson!' hissed Holmes, grasping my arm. 'That would explain the unknown names on the envelopes if we were to assume that they are victims of the blackmailing scheme. It would also suggest some reason as to why a stranger should burn Mr Addleton's papers, if that stranger too were a victim. And when a blackmailer disappears without trace, we must invariably fear the worst.'

'But what has happened to him?'

Holmes rose swiftly, and pulled me to my feet. 'As to that, the small volume which I recommended to Hopkins should bring that excellent young man to our side in a very few moments. I am an omnivorous reader, Watson, and there is no mystery in the word 'tumuli'. But come! Time is short.'

He led me further into the woods. The sound of the sea rose to our ears, and I was reminded irresistibly of the excellent descriptions which had so often thrilled me in Clark Russell's stories. There was something magical about the sound, which made my heart race with desire to learn the untold wonders of the ocean.

My musings were rudely interrupted, however, by the clear and rational voice of Sherlock Holmes. He had stopped us in our tracks and put his finger to his lips in thought.

'Have you ever heard of such a thing as a burial barrow, Watson?' said he.

Indeed I had. My knowledge of them was limited, but I knew that ancient civilizations were often known to bury tribal chiefs in tombs, whose location was then marked as a sign of respect with a mound of earth and a large pile of stones. They were then given a name that would befit the chief to whom the burial site was dedicated. Some barrows still remained in England, and were of some considerable size, although the locations of them were unknown to me. I said as much to Holmes, who nodded in appreciation.

'Your knowledge is basic,' said he, 'but sufficient for our purposes. Let me expand a little. The excellent book, which I gave Hopkins from Mr Addleton's own collection, was a history of ancient customs. One chapter was dedicated to burial rites, and within that chapter I found a very interesting piece of information. The ancient Romans were frequent users of the rite of the burial barrow, and many of the great leaders of Rome were buried in them. The official Roman name for them was . . . *tumuli*. The term was familiar to me, and I recognized it as soon as I saw Hopkins's reproduction of the message on the blotter. There were gaps in my knowledge, however, and at the time I could see no reason to connect a burial barrow with the case.

'However, contained within the book I found in Addleton's study, was mention of a burial barrow, which still exists in this country, by the name of the Giant's Hand. And where do you think this barrow is, Doctor?' His eyes gleamed with excitement as he spoke, and the answer to his question was obvious to me.

'Within the grounds of Malvere Towers!'

'Precisely! Indeed, Doctor, according to the book, it should be — ! Ha! Do you see it, Watson?'

I followed his thin forefinger as he pointed into the distance. My eyes fell upon the object before us, and widened in amazement. In a clearing in the trees I saw a huge length of earth, built into a mound, and of a size I would not dare to estimate. It seemed to stretch the whole width of the clearing, and so awesome was it that the impression was that it could have continued beyond. Stones and rocks ran along the top of the mound, like some sort of crown or head-dress, and completed the incredible effect that this construction had upon me. I had seen reproductions of such barrows in magazines, of course, but nothing could have prepared me for the reality.

'Behold,' said Sherlock Holmes softly, 'the Giant's Hand!'

We moved towards it, and built into the front of the mound of earth we saw a small archway, which formed an entrance to the barrow. This was boarded up with wood and stone, and, as we approached it, Sherlock Holmes threw himself upon his knees, whipped out his lens and began to examine the opening in the earth.

'I see now what attracted this historian to Malvere Towers,' I observed, staring up at the Giant's Hand as it loomed over my head. It seemed to brush the very sky.

'Indeed,' murmured Holmes. 'The attraction of such a historical find would have been irresistible to him.'

Suddenly, he let out a cry of satisfaction, and pulled me down to my knees. He pointed at the soil in front of the wood and stones which he had been examining, and I saw that there were smooth patches in the earth, which indicated that some heavy object had been dragged across the opening. Further examination revealed still more of such traces, and Holmes's eyes sparkled with excitement.

'These stones and pieces of wood have recently been moved,' he said. 'The last people to enter this particular tumuli need not necessarily have been dressed in togas and laurel wreaths! Come, Watson, help me shift these stones.'

It was not unduly heavy work, but I confess that there were beads of sweat forming on my brow by the time we had finished. Behind the stones that we had moved there was an opening made out of stone, which was almost too narrow for us to fit through. The light outside was beginning to show signs of fading now, and the rising darkness made the gloom beyond this stone door even more foreboding. Sherlock Holmes struck a match, and peered into the blackness. He indicated the area around the stone entrance.

'No cobwebs,' said he. 'Surely one would expect some evidence of the passing of time? It is further proof that somebody has entered this barrow recently.'

He took a step forward and bade me to follow. The ground beneath my feet was dry and dusty, and from the light of Holmes's match I could see that the earth was like sand. A harsh wind had whipped up outside and it whistled fiercely through the doorway by which we had entered. I have faced many examples of danger and threat in my adventurous life, but walking through that ancient barrow of death filled me with as much apprehension and nervousness as anything I have experienced before. Holmes walked slowly, and I could see by the light that he held that his face was pale and exultant, and his lips compressed in uncertainty.

For what seemed like an eternity we walked through that narrow, dusty corridor. Finally, however, we came upon a large chamber, which was clearly the main burial chamber of the barrow. The ceiling extended far above our heads, and its physical shape we were unable to see. Blackness seemed to descend upon us, and it was not difficult to imagine the stones, which seemed to brush the heavens from the outside, stretching up above us. This chamber was indeed a fitting tribute to any leader who would have been laid to rest here, so many centuries ago. Indeed, as the match Holmes held in his hand flickered and died, I caught sight of a huge marble tomb in the shape of a warrior, holding a large broadsword and a magnificent shield which bore a standard I could not recognize. It was a sobering thought that somewhere, beneath the pomp and circumstance of that marble tomb, there lay — in the very same antechamber in which I stood — the mortal remains of a once great and worthy man. At the foot of the tomb, there was something else that I would have then seen had the whole chamber not been plunged into utter darkness.

Holmes's match had died, and I heard him curse. He fumbled around in his pocket for another, and as quickly as it had come, the darkness was gone, as the match flickered and sparked into life. From the light of it, I saw at last what it was that had caught my eye at the foot of the tomb. I stared at it, and then at Holmes, whose face was expressionless, as though he had expected to find it there from the outset.

'There, Watson,' said he, 'is Mr Stanislaus Addleton.'

Before us lay the body of a middle-aged man, dressed in an evening suit and topcoat. His face was lean and ferret-like, and there was a neatly trimmed moustache adorning his upper lip. He had the characteristic, round shoulders of the academic and a large forehead that seemed to indicate the intelligence which would have once thrived within it. His hair was remarkable in its intensity of colour, and recalled to my mind the black moustache of Raymond Addleton, which certainly seemed to prove the relationship between them. He wore an expression of intense pain, and it was not difficult to perceive the cause of it, for protruding from his chest, like a terrible insignia, was a wooden-handled letter opener, stained with blood.

I overcame my initial shock at the sight and kneeled beside the body. From the state of the corpse, it was evident that he had been dead some time, and the fact that he had been murdered the previous night was undeniable. I said as much to Holmes, who struck another match in haste. 'Blackmail becomes murder, my dear Watson,' said he.

'The death certainly seems to support your theory about Mr Addleton's business ideas,' I replied. 'But who could do such a thing as this?'

'You ought to be able to deduce that for yourself,' replied my friend. 'There is only one person capable of such a crime as this. You know my methods, Watson.

Arrange each of the facts as we know them, and you will no doubt reach the correct conclusion.'

I was about to reply when something stopped me. In the distance I heard the sound of a boot against stone, and then footsteps growing ever nearer. I looked at Holmes, who evidently had heard it too, for he blew out the match and grabbed me by the arm. We moved over to the entrance to the chamber, and stood to one side. We stared ahead of us, down the passageway through which we had walked earlier, uncertain who was about to issue from it. I could see the glimmer of a lantern, and by its light was able to make out the figure of a man walking towards us. I felt Holmes's hand curl around mine and grasp it tightly.

For what seemed like an age, but which could only have been a few moments, the footsteps continued to move towards us, and suddenly the chamber was filled with light from a lantern, which was held aloft. Our eyes were blinded for a moment by the shock of the illumination, and I could only make out the outline of a tall man, wearing what seemed to be a bowler hat. Instinctively, my hand reached for my revolver, but Holmes's voice calmed me. His eyes must have become accustomed to the glare more rapidly than mine, for he had recognized the intruder at once.

'There is no need for violence, Watson,' said he.

'Indeed not!' said a familiar voice, and at last I recognized the man as being Inspector Hopkins.

'I am pleased that you saw the significance of that interesting volume, which I recommended to you,' remarked Holmes.

'Yes, indeed,' replied the inspector. 'I should never have found this place without your help, Mr Holmes. But how is it that neither Raymond Addleton nor his sister knew about it?'

'They most probably did,' answered Holmes. 'But they did not know what the word tumuli meant. It is hardly in common usage. Why, then, when a detective asks about tumuli should they connect it with the ancient barrow in the woods?'

'I take your point,' said Hopkins.

'The more interesting question,' continued Sherlock Holmes, moving away from us, 'is what do you make of that, Inspector?'

He pointed at the corpse lying in front of the warrior's tomb. With a gasp, Hopkins rushed towards it and stared down at its terrible visage. 'It is Mr Addleton,' said he. 'But who could have done this?'

'We shall turn our minds to that presently,' said Holmes. 'Watson tells me that he has been dead for some hours. Do you stand by that, Doctor?'

'Certainly,' I replied. 'He was murdered some time last night.'

'And since he was seen leaving the house at half past eleven, and it took Watson and me almost twenty minutes to get here, we might do worse than assume midnight to be a likely time of death.'

Hopkins had been examining the letter opener during Holmes's discourse, and when my friend had finished speaking, the inspector let out a gasp of excitement.

'This letter opener is from the study, I am sure of it!'

'How so?' asked Holmes.

'Did you not observe the many envelopes which had been so neatly opened?' returned Hopkins with some pride. 'And yet no trace of an implement was there. Surely this is that very instrument!'

Holmes clapped the official on the shoulder. 'Excellent, Hopkins! You scintillate this afternoon! I think your deduction is almost certainly correct. If you will excuse me for a moment, I should like to satisfy myself as to one point.'

He leaned over Hopkins, and stared intently at the corpse. The inspector shifted his weight and rose to stand beside me. Holmes knelt down, his face inches away from the corpse's hideous countenance, and he examined minutely the handle of the terrible weapon that burst forth from the man's chest. Hopkins looked at me with some measure of admiration in his eyes. I could not help but smile in agreement, for although I had seen Holmes at work so many times in the past there was something comforting in knowing that he was present, and that he had the situation firmly within his grasp.

'It is a pity that there are no footprints,' remarked Hopkins, staring at the floor. 'In this dust they would have proved invaluable.'

'The criminal must have obliterated them as best he could,' I replied.

'We will not need any footprints,' remarked Holmes. 'You have both overlooked a clue of the utmost importance yonder.'

He walked over to us and knelt down at our feet. He picked up a small cigarette stub, which he held aloft in his gloved hand. Hopkins examined it closely. 'It is a common enough brand,' said he.

'It seems to have most unusual qualities,' said I.

'Ha! What do you notice, Watson?' asked Holmes eagerly.

'It seems to be pinched all around the bottom.'

'Excellent!'

'But what does that mean?' asked

Stanley Hopkins, as Holmes handed him the cigarette stub.

Holmes's eyes glistened with triumph. 'It means that we have our case, Inspector. We require only a few missing links, and the matter is complete.'

He walked off towards the corridor through which we had entered, but paused and turned back to face us. 'By the by, do you notice anything peculiar about the corpse?'

We looked back at that dreadful sight. The handle of the letter opener, the terrible contortion of pain on the face, the outstretched hands pleading for help: all these things impressed themselves upon me once more, but I knew that it was not to any of them that Sherlock Holmes referred. We looked back at him and both shrugged out shoulders.

'Then I draw your attention, gentlemen, to the singular circumstance of the fourth button on Mr Addleton's waistcoat.'

Hopkins and I moved towards the corpse and looked at his chest. He wore a waistcoat of white satin, and the buttons glinted at us like tiny pearls lined down his breast. However, between the third and fifth, there was only a ragged tear.

'There is no fourth button!' we exclaimed.

'That is the singular circumstance,' remarked Sherlock Holmes, as he walked out into the fresh air.

★   ★   ★

I need not go into details of the formalities that we went through with regards to the removal of the body, nor of how we broke the news of Mr Addleton's tragic death to his family. It was Holmes who did so, and he managed it with that remarkable tact and gentleness which was characteristic of him. Dr Tewson was a comfort to the young couple, and Holmes declared that there was no further work for us to do that day. Hopkins informed us that he had taken rooms at a local inn the previous day and we accompanied him to them, leaving behind the tragedy of Malvere Towers.

During our drive, the inspector pressed

my companion for further details of his observations of the day, but Holmes remained silent, and to each of Hopkins's questions, he simply placed his finger to his lips. 'The time will come for explanations,' said he. 'There is a small enquiry which I wish to make in London, and if it proves successful then by tomorrow afternoon you shall have your man under lock and key.'

And no more would he say. We alighted at a small, cosy-looking inn designed after the fashion of the Tudors. Wisteria grew in excess across the front of the building, and a small wooden door was slightly ajar. A nameplate was mounted on the wall, which read 'The Crossing Gate', although there was no evidence of such to be seen, and through one of the windows came the flickering glare of a warm log fire. We could hear genial laughter from within, and after the darkness which surrounded the manor house not so far away, the sound was as welcome to me as a lighthouse is to troubled sea travellers.

'These are my lodgings,' said Hopkins. 'I look forward to hearing from you both tomorrow.'

'You shall certainly hear from me, Hopkins,' said Holmes, shaking the inspector's hand. 'But there is no need to say farewell to Watson here, for he is staying with you.'

I stared at my companion in amazement, and opened my mouth to protest, but Holmes shrugged his shoulders in his easy manner. 'After all, Doctor,' said he, 'there is no sense in wasting time and expense on a trip to London, when you will only have to return again tomorrow.'

'But our enquiries in London?' I stammered.

'There is no help you can give me there,' said Holmes. 'The inspector here will, I am sure, see you fit with a clean collar and an unused razor, and the Crossing Gate breakfasts will no doubt meet your expectations. Good-bye!'

And with that, he leaped back into the dogcart and rattled off into the distance. The hour now was fairly late, and there was a chill wind blowing, so with a shrug, the inspector and I made our way into the inn and I booked myself into a room. Fortunately, the landlady had a spare chamber adjacent to Hopkins's own, and so I signed the register at once.

Hopkins and I spent a most pleasant evening together. We talked about all manner of subjects, from past cases that had drawn us together, to investigations that Hopkins had seen through without the aid of my talented companion. He was full of admiration for Holmes and spoke at length about his fascination for the amateur's talents and his hope to develop his own abilities, with Holmes as his tutor. I had never spent such time alone with the young man before, and it was a pleasure to see someone so young with such enthusiasm for his subject. Finally, we finished the evening with a game of chess over a brandy, and retired to our rooms rather later than we had intended.

Sherlock Holmes was correct in his conjecture concerning the breakfast, and both Hopkins and I ate heartily. It was over our coffee that our conversation turned to the Addleton tragedy, and the contents of that ancient barrow.

'I cannot see where Mr Holmes is heading in his case,' confessed Hopkins.

'He seems to have very clear ideas.'

'I have seen him do a good many things, Doctor, but this case beats the lot. What is all this talk about watch chains and waistcoat buttons?'

'I cannot imagine.'

'No doubt there is a very good reason for them.'

I nodded. 'And no doubt Holmes will communicate with us as soon as he can.'

This was sooner than I had expected, for later that morning there arrived a telegram from my friend, which was addressed to me and ran as follows:

CASE COMPLETE. ALL EVIDENCE TO HAND. WILL RETURN MALVERE TOWERS BY NOON TRAIN

Hopkins was delighted by the news. 'Wonderful!' he cried, gripping the telegram in his hands. 'We shall meet him at the station!'

We waited on the platform, as Hopkins had suggested, and the train pulled in on time. As the steam from the engine chimney swirled around us like the thickest London fog, we heard the opening and closing of so many carriage doors. Then, through the steam, there appeared the tall, spare figure of Sherlock Holmes, dressed in his long travelling coat and his ear-flapped cap. We all three shook hands, and set off once more for Malvere Towers.

Hopkins was bursting with energy, and I could see from his tight lips and clenched fists that it was a struggle for him to keep silent. However, his experiences must have taught him that Holmes would not speak until he was ready, and I knew perfectly well that any attempt at seeking information from him would be futile. So it was that we sat in silence in that rickety dogcart, until at last we approached the gates of the house once more.

Muir answered the door to us, and Hopkins and I walked ahead of Holmes into the hallway. My friend stopped, however, and put his lips to Muir's ear. He whispered something, and the small butler pointed to the drawing room. Holmes nodded and walked with determination to the door of the room. 'Our quarry is in here,' he said grimly.

He opened the door and we entered. There was only one occupant of the room, and he was sitting in a large armchair in the corner, smoking a cigarette and reading a book, which was upon his lap. As we entered he looked up and smiled in greeting.

'Gentlemen,' said he, 'what news do you bring?'

Sherlock Holmes walked forward and stood over him. 'We bring news of a noose for your neck, Doctor,' said he with some considerable pride.

Dr Eustace Tewson was silent for a moment and then he rose with a chuckle. 'Really, Mr Holmes, I was quite impressed by your powers yesterday but now you do show yourself to be rather foolish.'

'I think not,' said Holmes, unmoved by the doctor's mockery.

'Then you accuse me of the murder of

my best friend of many years?' exclaimed Dr Tewson.

'I accuse you of the murder of the man who was blackmailing you about the death of Alice Barclay, a wealthy spinster, whose fortune you inherited after supplying her with an overdose of a sleeping draught.'

There was silence. Dr Tewson poured himself a glass of whisky, and stared out of the window. It was clear to us all that he was never going to speak of his own accord, and so Sherlock Holmes sat on the arm of the settee and began a most remarkable narrative.

'I shall tell you the facts upon which my conclusions are based, Doctor,' said he, 'and you can tell me if anything I say is erroneous. The first point of significance was the message, which Inspector Hopkins found on the blotter in the study, and which clearly indicated a pre-arranged meeting. The mention of the word tumuli alerted me at once, for it is a term familiar to me as meaning burial barrows. It is an advantage in the art of detection to have a wide knowledge of all subjects, for one never knows when that knowledge may be of some use. There had, however, been no mention of a burial barrow in connection with the disappearance with Mr Addleton, but I felt sure that in time I would find such a barrow near here.

'The second point about the message was the use of the term 'instalment' and the mention of the name Barclay. As I have explained to my friend, Dr Watson, this wording and the envelopes I found addressed to complete strangers assured me in my own mind that Addleton was a blackmailer. The papers which had been emptied from the safe, remnants of which I found in the fire grate, must surely have been documents relating to the black-mailing scheme. If so, it might explain why nobody but Mr Addleton had a combination to the safe, since he would naturally not wish his 'occupation' to be known, and so the contents of the safe had to be kept away from prying eyes. I had surmised so far when it struck me how extraordinary it would be for a blackmailer to burn his own proof of his victim's indiscretions. Of course the idea is preposterous, and so I conjectured that the papers had in fact been burned by someone else — indeed, by a victim of the blackmail.

'I had got so far in my thoughts, when I came upon a clue of the very first importance and one which hinted for the first time at the guilty party. This was the pocket watch, supposedly left behind by Mr Addleton; and the singular damage to one of the rings on the chain. The ring was twisted and although I pointed the fact out to him, I fancy that Inspector Hopkins failed to see the significance.'

'I must confess to it,' said the official.

'The point is,' continued Holmes, 'that the ring had been damaged, and we had heard that the watch was an heirloom. It was unlikely, therefore, that Mr Addleton would have been careless enough to leave it behind, and impossible to suppose that he would damage it himself. Thus, someone else must have damaged it, and the twisted link on the chain indicated that it had been wrenched from Mr

Addleton's pocket. The missing button on his waistcoat, which showed that the watch had once been there but had been removed with some violence, supported this supposition. This point was also, I fear, lost on Hopkins, although I hope that he sees its relevance now. Before I had left the study, therefore, I had ascertained several points. I was convinced that Mr Addleton was a blackmailer, and that the papers had been burned by one of his victims to hide the fact. I was also convinced that this second person was inside the house. Why else would they take the watch unless it was for the use of the key which hung from it? There had been a meeting, the murder was committed, and the murderer, in panic, pulled the watch from his victim's pocket. He returned to the house and let himself in, unaware that the butler had heard the door close.

'I had already formed a theory that it was you, Dr Tewson, who was guilty, but the true facts of the matter came to light only when I entered the burial barrow. There I found the corpse of Mr Addleton, stabbed with his own letter opener, which again indicated that the killer was to be found within the household. Furthermore, I found a cigarette stub that had, as Watson observed, some distinct characteristics.'

'It was pinched all around one end,' I recalled.

'Precisely. And then I remembered that upon our first meeting, Dr Tewson, you were smoking a cigarette through a holder, as indeed you are now. If we remove that cigarette from the holder, I am sure that we will see a similar, pinched effect upon that stub as upon the one you so carelessly left behind. That stub placed you beyond doubt in the barrow, and the finger of guilt pointed directly at you. You mentioned that Addleton had spoken to you about tumuli in the past, and therefore it was possible that you knew what the word meant.

'You arranged the meeting and you met in the barrow so as to avoid any disturbance. You knew that such a fanatical historian as Addleton would not have been able to resist the temptation of seeing inside the barrow that he loved so dearly, and so there was no difficulty in luring him there. You took the letter opener and joined him. After a short interview, during which the cigarette was smoked, murder was done. You took the watch, but your fingers were shaking and you had to resort to wrenching it loose. But you hoped that no one would ever find the body, so it did not really matter. You returned to the house, letting yourself in with the key on the watch chain, and retired to bed, having burned the papers in the fire.'

'But why?' asked Hopkins suddenly. 'What motive is there?'

'The blackmail,' said Holmes. 'During my visit to London I went to Doctors' Commons and found out about Dr Tewson's past life. He was listed as a wealthy man, having earned his money from a legacy left to him by an elderly patient named Alice Barclay. A little research in the back issues of *The Times* told Miss Barclay's story well enough. She had altered her will, leaving all her fortune to her personal medical adviser of many years. Only a few weeks after doing so, she died from an overdose of a sleeping draught. It was believed to have been an accident, but to blackmail a man about an accident was unthinkable. Alice Barclay was murdered, as surely as Stanislaus Addleton, and by the same man. Is that not so, Dr Eustace Tewson!'

Sherlock Holmes fell silent, and allowed the effect of his words to sink into the atmosphere. Dr Tewson turned upon his heel and paced over to my companion. He held out his hand with a smile. 'I repeat what I said yesterday, Mr Holmes. The reports of your powers are not exaggerated. You are a remarkable man.'

Holmes looked at the outstretched hand before him. He rose, placed his cap upon his head and, with a nod to Hopkins, walked out of the room.

★　★　★

There is little more for me to say. A few months later, we read of the trial of Dr Eustace Tewson for the murders of Alice Barclay and Stanislaus Addleton. He was found guilty of both charges, and sentenced to death by hanging. The report had prompted me to look over my notes once more, and I came across a point that Holmes had failed to explain. We were seated beside the fire in Baker Street, and I put the question to him that had been puzzling me.

'How did Dr Tewson gain access to the combination of the safe?' I asked. 'There was nobody in the house who knew it.'

Sherlock Holmes smiled. 'Nor did he. The answer to that problem, Watson, is simplicity itself, and once I had grasped the idea, I saw that Dr Tewson was the only possible culprit. He did not know the combination, but he was able to discover it.'

'How so?'

'By using an implement which only a doctor could have easily obtained. The answer to your puzzle, Doctor, is in your top hat.'

I frowned in bewilderment, and walked over to our hatstand. I took down my glossy top hat and felt inside. My hand fell at once upon an instrument which I use every day in my medical capacity. I smiled as it did so, and looked over at Sherlock Holmes.

'A stethoscope,' said I.

'Precisely,' he replied. 'I myself have been known to break into safes using that very piece of medical equipment. It is surprising how effective they are. And now, Watson, if you would be good enough to engage Mrs Hudson, I am quite ready for some tea. And then, I should like you to read this letter which arrived this morning. It promises to be a most interesting case, should we decide to turn our attention to the singular problem of the Ambleside Resurrection.'

The Adventure of the York Place Prophecy

I have remarked elsewhere that of all the problems submitted before my friend, Mr Sherlock Holmes, during the years of our association, there were only two which I was the means of introducing to his notice. The first, that of Mr Hatherley's thumb, I have published already, but the second, the affair of Colonel Warburton's madness, was of such a delicate nature that until now, ten years since it occurred, publication has been impossible. A pledge of secrecy was made at the time to the colonel's daughter, a pledge from which I have only recently been freed by the untimely death of Miss Elise Warburton. It is perhaps fortunate that I should now choose to bring the matter to light, for, country gossip being what it is, there are unpleasant rumours as to the facts of the matter, which tend to make the case more terrible than the truth.

It was in the spring of 1889 that I was seated at my desk writing up a few patients' reports. I had, at this time, abandoned Holmes in his Baker Street rooms and had returned to civil practice in Paddington, so that I saw little of my companion at this time, for I was kept rather busy. Since my practice was not too far from the station, I was often able to give assistance to the officials. One of these, whom I had cured of a painful disease, was never weary of advertising my virtues, and would do so to his colleagues and friends. It was from him that I got to hear of the Reverend Alistair Craddock, whose tale brought us into contact with the case of Colonel Warburton's madness.

I was seated at my desk, then, when Mary Jane, the maid, began tapping at the door. She entered and was followed by a small, wiry man of sixty, whose wispy hair and lined face told of many stories and spoke of volumes of experience in life. His shoulders were rounded and his knees were bent, as much from some terrible weight upon his conscience as from his declining years. He was introduced as the Reverend Alistair Craddock, and as he stepped forward into the light, I saw that he held a bloodstained handkerchief up to his head. I thanked Mary Jane and asked her to leave us alone.

'I am sorry to trouble you, Doctor,' said my visitor, apologetically. 'The fact is that I got your name from a guard at Paddington, who suggested that I came to see you. I was on his train, you see, just after this happened.' He lifted the handkerchief to reveal a large, discoloured lump upon his forehead. It was evidently a fresh wound, for it had only recently stopped bleeding, and was of such a depth for me to realize that some force was behind the blow which had inflicted it.

I reached for my medical supplies, cleaned and sponged the wound, and finally wrapped a bandage around my patient's head. A small crimson patch began to soak through it, as the remaining blood became apparent.

'When did this happen?' I asked,

handing the reverend gentleman a glass of water.

'This morning,' he replied. 'I had only recently risen when I was attacked from behind, clubbed and left — one supposes — for dead. When I came to, I did what I could for myself. However, I had not the time to worry about it, for I had business in town and so came up without first having received medical attention.'

'That was a little foolish.'

He nodded wisely. 'I realize that, but at the time, as you may imagine, I was not thinking rationally. Indeed, even now, my head throbs uncontrollably.'

I checked his wound again, to ensure that the bandage was secure, and assured him that the wound would heal in time. I was, however, intrigued by his story, which had whetted my appetite for mystery and had set off a train of thought in my mind.

'Did you see who it was that attacked you?' I asked. 'Can you supply a motive for the incident? Has anything been stolen, for example?'

The vicar shook his head, and gulped

the remainder of his water. 'As to motive, I have no clue. But I know full well who attacked me.'

'Who?'

'It was my friend and neighbour, Colonel Jeremiah Warburton.'

I started at his certainty. 'How can you be so sure?'

The vicar's voice sank almost to a whisper, and his eyes twitched with anxious emotion.

'For the simple reason, Doctor, that he has attacked me four times before!'

As my visitor spoke, my heart began to race and I thought of Holmes, and how the nature of the problem was just the sort to appeal to him. It was when the Reverend Craddock began to speak of informing the police of the attack that I put forward my idea.

'May I suggest,' said I eagerly, 'that if it is anything in the nature of a mystery which you would wish to see solved, that you speak to my friend, Mr Sherlock Holmes, before you go to the official police?'

He seemed pleased with my suggestion,

and said that if Mr Holmes would be interested in the case, he would be glad to speak to him. And so it was that within five minutes, we were in a hansom together, rattling *en route* to Baker Street.

As we entered the familiar sitting room, Sherlock Holmes was sitting at his chemical desk, working hard over an experiment. His long thin back, draped in the old dressing gown that I knew so well, was bent over a boiling retort and a Bunsen burner. For a second or two he seemed oblivious to our presence, despite my calling him twice. Finally, the experiment concluded with a fierce belch and a foul smell, and he gave a cry of triumph and rose.

'Sorry to keep you, Watson,' said he, shaking me warmly by the hand. 'It was important that I concluded the experiment if I am to solve the horror of the Lambeth beetle, a story for which even you are not prepared.'

He moved over to the window and threw it wide to clear the room of the pungent smell of the smoke, and then turned his attention to the Reverend

Craddock. Observing the bandaged head of the vicar, he ordered a large plate of ham and eggs and, upon their arrival, he joined us in a hearty meal. When we had finished, he settled our new acquaintance on the sofa, placed a pillow beneath his head, and laid a carafe of water and a glass within his reach.

'Pray make yourself at home, sir,' said he. 'Tell us what you may, but rest when you feel tired.' He settled down in his armchair, and placed his fingertips together. 'I trust that you do have a problem and that Watson has not brought you here in a social capacity.'

Our visitor shuffled uneasily on the sofa, as much from confusion as from discomfort. 'Well, yes, I do have a problem, Mr Holmes, upon which I should value your advice. I simply cannot believe that Colonel Jeremiah Warburton has gone mad, and yet his behaviour of late does give me cause for concern.

'You should know that I am vicar to the parish of a small village on the outskirts of Chislehurst in Kent. I have a healthy congregation, all of whom are regular visitors to the church. I am not saying that it would not be nice to see certain faces more than once or twice a year, but on the whole, the people of my parish are loyal and faithful. One family in particular has been with me for many years: Jeremiah Warburton and his daughter, Elise.

'I have known Warburton for twenty years or so, ever since I baptized his daughter in my church. Her mother had died in childbirth, alas, and her death was a severe blow to the colonel for he was devoted to Elizabeth. She always said that if she departed this life first, the colonel would break down. Recent events have proved her to be correct.'

'Pray, be precise as to details,' said Sherlock Holmes.

'Not to be blunt about it, Mr Holmes, for I am not one for gossip and do not wish to add to it, but Warburton has been behaving very strangely recently, and it has led to the more idle tongues in our village to believe that the old colonel is mad. He seems to have lost whatever keen senses he once had. The precise chronology of events is of the utmost importance, I think, and so I shall be as exact as possible.

'Two months ago, there came to the parish a stranger. Mr Sebastian Dorey came to live in Lowrey Cottage, a sixteenth-century farmhouse. He made regular visits to my church and would often spend long days sitting at the altar, gazing up at the carved crucifix which adorns it, but always, it seemed to me, with a look of anguish upon his face. It took some time for Mr Dorey to settle, but eventually he did so, and became closely acquainted with Colonel Warburton and his daughter. Dorey was invited to dinner at Warburton's house, York Place, along with myself, and his daughter. It was a cheery affair, during which the colonel talked about past campaigns and his decorations. He told of his involvement in the Indian Mutiny, for he had played a great part in the campaign at Lucknow, and was closely associated with Sir Colin Campbell, Lord Clyde. He spoke of Elise and his hopes for her education. She is showing great promise in her studies of art, and is quite an accomplished painter, Mr Holmes. York Place is filled with her work, some of which rival the Masters themselves.

'After dinner, we retired to the drawing room, although the colonel said he had some business to attend to in his study, and would join us presently. He returned his usual self, and we passed a pleasant evening. It was exactly a week ago today, however, that the change came over him that has left him the quivering wreck he is now. Exactly what happened is not clear to me, for I heard it from Elise, who is herself at the end of her nerves.

'She came to see me that day and it was clear that some great tragedy had occurred. Never have I seen such a terrified glare in the girl's eyes, Mr Holmes! It seemed as if the devil himself had appeared before her. She suffers, it seems, from some degree of insomnia, an affliction inherited from her late mother. That night, the night of the dinner, she slept fitfully and rose to fetch a glass of water. As she left her room, she heard a heated quarrel downstairs, involving her father. She could hear his voice distinctly. The other voice was muffled, but she is certain that it was none other than Mr Sebastian Dorey.

'The next morning, she questioned her father, whose appearance had changed overnight, and who now looked so haggard and grey, when once he had been noble and elegant. His reply was that his affairs were no concern of a girl barely out of school, and that she ought to mind her own business or learn to regret it. Naturally, this upset Elise very much, for this man was not her father, who was caring and devoted. A complete change had come over him. He refused to come to church and has not spoken to me since that night, a week ago.

'It seemed to me that the change had occurred as a result of the quarrel with Mr Dorey. Hence, I went to see him but was told that it did not concern me, and I should leave my interference in the pulpit. Matters came to a head just three days ago, however, when events took a turn for the worse.'

Sherlock Holmes had listened most

carefully to this narrative, delivered by the vicar between short sips of water. Holmes now opened his eyes and stared at his visitor.

'What exactly has occurred?' he asked.

The Reverend Craddock shuffled and glanced around the room with some anxiety. 'I rise early, and am often up and about before daybreak. Three days ago, I was about my business in the vicarage as usual, when I heard a loud banging noise outside, similar to a blade against wood. I went outside to investigate and was walking down the short path that leads from the vicarage to the church, when I saw Jeremiah Warburton in his night-shirt and dressing gown. He held a shovel in his hands, and was hammering it fiercely against the church door.

'I called after him, and on hearing my voice, he looked up at me and stopped his bizarre occupation. It was not so much his activity that unsettled me, but his face. He looked like no man on earth, but like a demon from the edges of the infernal abyss. His black hair was on end, billowing in the wind like the plumage of some wild raven; his eyes were wide, as though he had looked upon Hades itself. And yet it was not anger or madness that I read upon his face, Mr Holmes. It was *fear!*'

Holmes's brows knitted, and I could see that he was greatly excited. 'Your case is most interesting, and certainly promises to be unique. Did the colonel offer an explanation for his conduct?'

'I questioned him about it, of course, but he said nothing. He snarled viciously at me, threw aside his shovel and fled from me, as though time's chariot were at his heels.'

Holmes was silent for a moment. Presently, he indicated the vicar's bandaged head. 'Something else has occurred to bring you here today, has it not?'

'Indeed, Mr Holmes, and this is the unfortunate result. It came about in this way. I was pondering the events of the past week, for again I was up very early. I could not fathom it at all, for the colonel was a gentle man, and this savage attack on my church door had led to the rumours of his madness. They may yet be right.

'I had reached this conclusion when a large slab of stone hurtled through the church window, followed by another attack upon the door. I opened this and was faced with the wild countenance of Warburton. Suddenly, his hands were around my throat and I could feel my senses slipping away. Warburton took out his walking stick and struck me a blow to the head, leaving me insensible on the floor. When I recovered, I found my church in disarray. The carved crucifix of which I have spoken had been defaced and cut down, the altar destroyed and every depiction of Christ vandalized or annihilated. Such blasphemy I have never seen.'

'What says Colonel Warburton to these outrages?' I asked.

'He would not see me,' said the vicar, solemnly. 'Whenever he did, he would make an attack upon my life. It was useless to try to get any sense out of him, and so I gave up the attempt. I did what I could for my wound myself but had business in town that could not wait. I thought I was fit enough to come to London for the day, but I must have looked far worse than I thought, for upon my arrival at Paddington, the station guard directed me to Dr Watson, who brought me here to see you, Mr Holmes. I had hoped to keep the police out of the affair, but the continual attacks upon my person and my property must stop. And now, Mr Sherlock Holmes, you are in full possession of the facts. For God's sake, tell me your opinion of the matter. Is Colonel Jeremiah Warburton mad? What am I to do?'

For a moment or two there was silence, during which the vicar nursed his wound. I took a look at it myself and assured our visitor that it was healing well, and needed no immediate attention. Sherlock Holmes, however, sat perfectly still, his eyes tightly closed, looking to all who did not know him, as if he were asleep. I knew, however, that he was turning over in his head thought after thought and fact after fact.

'You told me,' said I at length, noting that my companion's silence unsettled the reverend gentleman, 'that Colonel War-burton had attacked you four times in all.'

'Indeed he has,' came the reply. 'They were not physical, however, for he was fought off by some neighbours before he could strike.'

'When were these attacks?' interjected Holmes suddenly.

'The first was the day after I disturbed his assault of the church door. I was passing a local inn, the Chislehurst Arms, when he came out and rushed at me. Albert Tennyson, the landlord, restrained him.'

'And the other assaults?'

'They all occurred in the next few days, culminating in this morning's affair, when he clubbed me and desecrated my church.'

'And these mad fits came upon him just after this argument with Mr Sebastian Dorey?' said Holmes.

'Yes.'

'And yet nobody knows what this argument was about?'

'None,' said the vicar grimly.

Holmes shook his head like a man who

is far from satisfied. 'This case is deeper and more subtle than we had at first supposed. Why should he attack the church so violently, and assault you — his friend — four times? He has attacked no one else in the parish?'

'That is so.'

'What can you tell us of Mr Dorey?'

The vicar shook his head, and his brows became knitted, as though the question was a difficult one. 'Very little, I am afraid,' said he. 'He came to our community two months ago, and keeps himself very much to himself. He is a private man of independent means, and is capable of the most eloquent speech.'

'Did he speak at Warburton's dinner?'

'He did.' The vicar's tone had changed from a sympathetic and genial one to one of reproachful scorn. 'He spoke of certain gifts that his mother had possessed. He claimed that she was able to predict the future, sometimes months in advance. It is all nonsense of course!'

I had expected Sherlock Holmes's cold yet admirably balanced mind would forbid him to accept such a notion and for him to reject it vigorously. And yet, he seemed indifferent to this startling revelation, and his eyes remained fixed upon his client, and his features rigid. Finally, he turned to me.

'What do you make of it all, Watson?'

'Precognitive visions? As a medical scientist, I am inclined to be sceptical,' said I.

A faint quiver of a smile flickered across Holmes's thin lips. 'We must not allow our vision of perception to be too limited, my dear Watson. There are, after all, more things in heaven and earth than are dreamt of in our philosophy. Several pieces have been written upon the subject of precognizance, in which it is claimed that the tendencies are inherited. If Mrs Dorey was so gifted, then it seems likely that her son is also.'

Alistair Craddock nodded. 'He claims to be a medium,' said he. 'More than once I have heard rumours of his apparent 'miracles'.'

Holmes was silent for a moment. 'I believe,' said he at last, 'that Mr Dorey's claim is of the utmost importance in this strange and tangled affair. Is the colonel fit now? How was he when you left?'

'He was gone when I came to. As far as I know, his madness has yet to subside.'

Holmes immediately led the vicar to the door. 'It is my belief that your friend is not mad, and that his behaviour is due to some other cause. As to what that cause may be I am at present unable to say. There are too many difficulties yet to be overcome. My advice to you is to carry out your business in town, as you had arranged, and then return to Chislehurst and begin rebuilding your life. Rest assured that Dr Watson and I shall come down to your parish tomorrow and look into this affair.'

With a few grateful words to us both, Alistair Craddock bade us farewell, and as he did so, I could not help but notice how his shoulders seemed less bowed and how the anxiety had eased in that troubled frame.

When he had gone, I turned to Sherlock Holmes. 'What is the meaning of it all?' I asked. 'Is there anything in this medium business?'

'Who can tell for certain?' he replied. 'But we must not rule out any possible explanation on the grounds of superstition. We must have evidence before we can form or discard theories. I must thank you for bringing a most interesting and unique case to my attention. It grows upon me, Watson, and I beg that you will not speak to me for at least an hour.'

With this, he curled himself up in his armchair, with his knees drawn up to his thin, hawk-like nose, and there he sat, his pipe thrusting out like the bill of a strange bird, and his eyes tightly closed. 'Why don't you go home, Watson, for we can be of little use to each other today. If you will be so good, I shall see you tomorrow at ten for breakfast, and we shall travel to Chislehurst together. And I say, Doctor, there may be some little danger, so put your service revolver in your pocket.'

* * *

The next morning found me at Baker Street at ten o'clock precisely. Breakfast had been laid out for me, and Holmes sat at the table, in his mouse-coloured dressing gown, deep in a study of *The Times*. The previous night, I had turned over in my head the events concerning Colonel Warburton but no satisfactory answer could I find to all the questions that plagued the affair. It seemed clear to me that no other explanation for the events was plausible, other than the hypothesis that the man was mad. Why else should he be close friends with Mr Craddock one day, yet viciously attack him the next? He had been a regular churchgoer, and yet, here he was, destroying his very place of worship. Surely it must be madness that so diseased him. And yet, my medical studies and my professional skill forbade me from accepting such a simple solution. I knew full well that no man could possibly lose his senses so completely and so rapidly. My training at the University of London had often concentrated upon psychological disease, and so I felt quite confident in making such an assumption. But what other solution? I cudgelled my brains to find some possible explanation, but in vain. I put my ponderings to Sherlock Holmes as we sat at the breakfast table, and he seemed appreciative and pleased with my efforts.

'Very good, Watson,' said he, with a smile. 'You sum up the difficulties succinctly and well. As you say, there is no possibility of a man being sane one night and insane the following morning. Hence, we must look elsewhere for an explanation.'

'But where?'

'Well, the man's actions are certainly unusual, and although they appear to be destructive, might they not also be *defensive*? A man may beat another, but only to safeguard his own life. Similarly, a man may destroy a church because he fears it, and not because he despises it. Remember, he once placed all his faith in it.

'Now we must ask ourselves *why* he fears it. On the night of the dinner party, he feared nothing. Then, he argues with this man, Sebastian Dorey, who claims to be a psychic medium. It is after this argument that the colonel becomes a different man.'

'So, it is whatever Mr Dorey said which has caused the fear,' I suggested.

'Bravo, Watson!' cried Holmes.

'That, then, is your theory?'

'It is my working hypothesis,' he replied, shaking his head. 'The distinction is clear. There are, at present, insufficient facts to construct a completely workable theory. Now, if you are ready, Watson, we shall leave for the Chislehurst train.'

A short ride in a hansom brought us to the station, on a breezy morning when the chill air, though fresh, bit into our cheeks. Some warm tea at the station thawed us, however, and we finally settled ourselves down in a first-class carriage, bound for our destination. We were met, upon our arrival, by Mr Craddock, who had brought his trap with him, and we drove a short distance to the vicarage.

After rattling down a series of narrow, country lanes, we found ourselves at a large park gate, which was opened by a small, fresh-faced lad. In front of us was a very large and ancient church, whose tall steeple spoke of many confessed sins, and which looked out over the town like the very eyes of God. Behind the church, in a very large park, was the vicarage house, bordered all around by ancient elms and beeches. It was drowned in ivy, which showed by its colour the care that was taken with it by its owner.

As we alighted from the trap, we heard a man's voice behind us. Turning round, we saw a tall, thin man, very handsome, but with the weather-beaten face that so often betrays a life of experience in the tropics. From his bearing and meticulous dress, I could see that he was, like myself, a military man. His face, however, was filled with great distress and his eyes were wide, his mouth agape.

'Craddock!' he cried. 'Who are these men?'

'Mr Sherlock Holmes and his colleague, Dr Watson,' said our client. 'This is Major Reginald Merridew, who served in the same regiment as Colonel Warburton. They fought many campaigns together, often becoming great rivals. But, my dear Merridew, what is the matter? What has happened?'

The vicar's words seemed to bring more horror into the man's face than was already apparent. It was some time before he could finally bring himself to answer, and when he did so, I felt a surge of ice-cold fear run down my spine, for there was a thrill in the major's voice that made the news more terrifying than the truth.

He stared at us, all three, and gasped: 'It is Colonel Warburton! He has been *murdered*!'

It was one of those dramatic moments for which my friend existed. I stared at him, his lips compressed and his brows drawn over his eyes. Mr Craddock sprang forward and grabbed the old campaigner by the hand.

'God help us! Is it true? Is it — ?'

Merridew nodded grimly. 'I am afraid so. He was found early this morning. I came to see you but you had gone out, and your maid had no idea when you would return.'

Sherlock Holmes stepped forward with an authoritative stride and stood between the two men. 'Where was the colonel found?' he asked.

Major Merridew looked at my companion in some surprise. It was evident that he found our presence unsettling. 'There is an isolated area of woodland behind York Place,' said he. 'Harvey, his batman, discovered the body there as he took a morning stroll. Look here, Craddock, I think you ought to see Elise about all this. She's terribly upset, you know, and your presence may have a steadying effect upon her.'

The old vicar nodded his head. 'Of course, of course!' he said. 'Mr Holmes, won't you accompany me?'

'I should be happy to do so,' replied my companion. 'If I might ask the major a question first? Is it certain that the colonel died an unnatural death?'

'When you see the body, Mr Holmes, you will answer that question for yourself.'

'Is it common knowledge that he is dead?'

'In a small community like this, few secrets are kept.'

We took Craddock's trap to York Place, the home of Colonel Warburton. It was a large, rambling house with two large turrets at either side. Large stone pillars, after the fashion of Palladio, framed the majestic entrance to the house, which was decorated with wisteria that seemed to possess a soul and character of its own. We were greeted at the door by a butler and a small man dressed in the style of a soldier's attendant. This, evidently, was Harvey, who had discovered the poor colonel's body.

We entered the house, and I was at once impressed by the dedication that Colonel Warburton had for his vocation. There was a fine collection of weapons and maps of old campaigns, no doubt to remind the colonel of his history, and of his many successes. Interspersed with these was a fine collection of watercolours, which were clearly the work of the daughter of the house, of whose skill the vicar had spoken at Baker Street. We were led from this hallway into a large room, where our attention was seized by a very fine portrait of an elderly man in military uniform. Craddock pointed to it.

'That is Colonel Warburton,' said he.

'Before the recent terrible events,' observed Holmes. 'The artist?'

'She stands beside it.'

Facing us was a dignified young woman, barely twenty years old. Her face was delicately formed, but possessed that keen nature and patrician poise that was so clearly demonstrated in the portrait. The relationship was clear. She stepped forward, her eyes still moist with recent tears.

'Mr Holmes?' said she, glancing from one to the other of us.

Holmes gave a brief nod. 'At your service. We share your loss, and hope to put aright as best we can any problems that may face you.'

She smiled, a faint flicker across her fine lips, as she tried bravely to keep her bearing. 'You are most kind. Mr Craddock said as much when he returned yesterday.'

'Have you informed the police of the tragedy?' I asked.

Elise Warburton turned to me, and I noted a glimpse of desperation in her eyes. 'You misunderstand, Doctor. The police have been here for two days.'

'How is that possible?' asked Holmes. 'As I understand the situation, your father's death was discovered this morning.'

Elise Warburton showed us to a settee, upon which we sat. Ordering some tea, she sat down before us and dabbed her glistening eyes with a handkerchief. 'Yesterday, when Mr Craddock went up to London, my father had already attacked him physically. That was the last the good vicar saw of him. Father came home in a furious rage, and bellowed at me to leave him alone, threatening to kill me if I ever went near him again. I saw fear in his eyes, Mr Holmes, like I have never seen before. He said he had some business with Mr Dorey, and he rushed out of the house. That was yesterday afternoon, and he did not return. I informed the police late last night and the local constable arrived, saying that he could do very little. He left me with no hope, save that he would keep his eyes open. This morning, Harvey went out for his usual walk in the woods and found father's body. He rushed home, told me and I informed the constable. He came instantly, and said that it would be a matter for Scotland Yard. An officer from there arrived only an hour before you did yourselves.'

Holmes sat for some time in silence, his chin resting upon his hands, and his grey eyes fixed upon the fireplace. Finally he rose, and turned to the door, where the major and our client stood. 'Where is the body now?' he asked.

'The police moved it to the outhouse at the bottom of the garden.'

Holmes turned back to Miss Warburton. 'You say that your father had business with Mr Dorey. Have you any idea of its nature?'

'None, Mr Holmes.'

'I believe you overheard a quarrel between your father and this man, Dorey?'

'That is so.'

'What was it about?'

'I do not know. I could only hear a muffled exchange between them, but it was very heated. I asked both my father and Mr Dorey but received no answer from either of them.'

We left the distressed girl in the company of the major and our client, and moved into the garden. Several constables were standing there, comparing notes and theories, and generally betraying the presence of Scotland Yard. The outhouse was a small building, which stood at the back of the extensive garden. Holmes was eager to get there, in order to examine the corpse, but he was stopped by the distant calling of his name. We turned around and saw Harvey, the batman, running after us.

'Mr Holmes! May I have a word? Are you going to help find out who did this to the poor colonel, sir?'

'I shall do my best, Harvey, I assure you,' said Holmes genially. 'Now tell me all that happened when you found the body. You had gone for a walk, I understand?'

The batman nodded. 'Yes, sir. I always take a stroll in the woods over there.' He pointed to a clearing of trees behind the house. 'It gets me started for the day. I was on my way back when I noticed something half buried in a ditch before me. I couldn't tell what it was, for it was wrapped in a cloth of some kind. When I moved closer, however, I was almost sick at the sight of what lay before me. It was the master, but with a look on him that I have never seen before. It was terrible to look upon!'

Holmes's eyes gleamed with excitement, and his lips quivered as Harvey spoke. I could see that the facts of the case were suitably unusual to satisfy his curiosity, and that the case was one of such complexity to please him.

'Who moved the body to the out-house?'

'The local constable and myself, sir. Major Merridew suggested his own outhouse, but this was nearer.'

'Ah!' said Holmes. 'That is very clear. If I can do anything in the way of solving this matter, Harvey, I shall let you know. Goodbye!' When the lad had departed, Holmes turned to me with a twinkle in his eye. 'You see the importance of that interview, Watson?'

'I confess that I see little of any relevance in what he told us.'

'Precisely,' said Holmes. 'You may *see* little of importance, but I *observe* a great deal in young Harvey's words.'

Our attention was diverted at this point by a familiar voice that made us both turn our heads. On doing so, we were greeted by the eager face of Inspector Lestrade, our companion of the Yard, who walked towards us with outstretched hands. 'Glad to see you both,' said he. 'I suppose you know all the facts as well as I, Mr Holmes, although I think that this time we may not need your services. It seems to me that this case is of a rather elementary nature.' He smiled at us slyly, and winked at us with some amusement.

'You have a theory then?'

The little official puffed out his chest with confidence. 'I think you might call it that, Mr Holmes, and no mistake. If you ask me, it's this chap Dorey we have to see. Plain as a pikestaff! It all fits. The colonel argues with him, goes out of his senses, and then tells the daughter he has 'business' with this fellow. That's the last anybody sees of the old colonel, and the next thing you know, he turns up dead. Yes! I don't believe we'll need you here today, Mr Sherlock Holmes!'

'Your case seems a little lacking in its credibility, Lestrade,' replied my friend. 'For example, what motive does Mr Dorey have for the murder?'

Lestrade shrugged his shoulders. 'Details, Mr Holmes, minor details! Once we have him behind bars, we'll have all the facts in our hands. I'm just off to see him now, if you would care to come along?'

Holmes shook his head. 'I think that first of all I should like to see the body, Lestrade, and then I shall be happy to accompany you to Mr Dorey's cottage to hear his story.'

Lestrade seemed uneasy at this suggestion, for he shuffled upon the spot and his eyes darted from one to the other of us. 'You may view the body by all means,' said he. 'But be warned. Prepare yourselves, for it is not a pretty sight. You and I have seen death together many times, Mr Holmes, each more terrible than the last, but nothing to compare with this.'

He turned on his heel and led us towards the outhouse, his words causing a cold sense of uncertain fear to run through our veins. As we entered the outhouse, I saw, lying on the floor, a large piece of tarpaulin, under which lay the body of the unfortunate colonel. As Lestrade lifted the covering, a feeling of nausea swept over me. I have seen death in many forms, but seldom has it appeared to me in a more fearsome aspect than in that dark outhouse. The body lay upon its back, its arms hanging loosely by its sides and the legs splayed like the limbs of a broken puppet. It was evident to trained eyes like my own that the legs had been broken viciously at the knees, but for what purpose I could not begin to imagine. The man who lay before us was like a distorted and grotesque caricature of the portrait that we had seen in the house. His grey hair was wildly unkempt, his sightless eyes stared wide, and his teeth were bared in a feral snarl. Never have I seen such a look of terror on a man's face, as though he had actually foreseen his own death.

Holmes knelt beside the body at once and examined the wrists. 'Lestrade, have you the time of death?'

'The local doctor puts it at about six o'clock this morning.'

'I would agree with that,' said I, 'judging from the rigidity of the muscles.'

'Quite so,' said Holmes. 'And yet death, it seems, would be welcome to this man. Have you observed his wrists, gentlemen?' He pushed back the cuff of the dead man's shirt and revealed patches of raw, bloodied skin. 'It would appear that our colonel has been tied up for some time. Watson, you note that the legs have been broken?'

'With some force.'

'What do you make of that?'

'There seems to be no reason for it.'

Holmes nodded. 'Precisely so, Doctor, and therefore we may conclude that there was some very definite reason for it. This murder has been committed by someone with a certain degree of intelligence, and intelligent murderers are seldom mindlessly violent. What was the cause of death, Inspector?'

Lestrade consulted his notebook. 'The doctor said that at first glance it would appear to be asphyxiation. The peculiar colour of his skin suggests a lack of air, and the absence of any cuts or wounds a lack of an actual weapon.'

'Harvey, the batman, says that he and the local constable moved the body from the woods to here. On your orders?'

'That is so.'

'And apart from those two, and ourselves, no one else has seen the body?'

'Indeed. Miss Warburton wanted to, but I refused.'

Holmes shook his head. 'This is a most peculiar crime, and the more I see of it the less I like it. Why should one man asphyxiate another, tie him up and then break his legs? Why not a simple bullet or a knife?'

Lestrade sighed. 'There's no accounting for the criminal mind. You know that as well as I, Mr Holmes.'

'There is a reason for everything, Lestrade. Random violence is seldom done for pleasure. But hello! What is this?'

He had been walking around the outhouse with his magnifying lens, and now he stopped at the far wall. Moving across to him, we saw that his attention had been seized by two hooks in the wall, which were some twelve feet off the ground. His immediate reaction was to send for Harvey, who came promptly.

'Do all the outhouses in this district have hooks similar to these, Harvey?' asked Holmes when the boy arrived.

'Yes, sir. I don't know what they are used for, but they all have them.'

'How can you be so certain?'

'My duties have often called for me to enter the outhouses for various tools or whatever, and I have frequently seen these hooks.'

'This is most interesting. Well, Lestrade,' said Holmes, when the batman had left, 'I think we can now visit Mr Sebastian Dorey.'

The man in question was about thirty years old, with dark, piercing eyes, and a face with the look of mistrust upon it. His eyes shifted all around in nervousness during the interview and it was clear that he resented our presence.

'I understand,' said Holmes, 'that you have . . . unusual qualities, Mr Dorey?'

Dorey shifted in his seat. 'Did you come here to mock an hereditary gift, Mr Holmes, or to find out more about it?'

My companion raised a hand in protest. 'I came for neither reason. Mr Craddock, your local vicar, asked me to look into the small matter of Colonel Warburton's strange behaviour.'

'His madness, you mean?' snarled Dorey in some contempt. Holmes made no reply. 'He was not mad,' continued the medium. 'He was the sanest of the lot around here. He *believed*, you see.'

'Believed what?' asked Lestrade, with some severity.

'The truth. I told him that he ought to fear the church, for it would end him somehow.'

'How would it do so?'

Dorey lowered his gaze in anxiety. 'I do not know. The vision was blurred. All I saw was the colonel's face atop a large, worm-eaten crucifix.'

Holmes gave a sudden cry of satisfaction, and we turned to look at him. I saw that his eyes were sparkling with triumph. 'Did your vision concern only the church?'

'Yes. Usually my visions are metaphorical, not literal, and take time to decipher. But this was only too clear to me. Warburton featured in it, and so it was obviously a warning to him and the future! The crucifix is a symbol in popular terms for religion and the church. I could only think that Craddock would in some way betray Warburton — or kill him.'

'Did you mention this to anyone?'

'Only Warburton. I attended his dinner party, and told him afterwards, when we were alone. He flew off the handle at me, telling me to mind my own business and keep my ridiculous stories to myself. I had no idea that his daughter had heard us quarrel.'

'What did you tell him?' Holmes's voice had become high and strident, which told me that he was greatly interested in the man's remarkable tale.

'What I have told you, Mr Holmes. I said that the church or Craddock meant him harm in some way. He ordered me out of the house, of course, but I could see that he believed it in his own mind. His eyes betrayed as much.'

Lestrade sniffed sardonically. 'And now he's dead, Mr Dorey! Did you see *that* in a dream? I think you have a lot to answer for!'

Holmes threw Lestrade a sharp glance. 'Nonsense! Would he have co-operated this much, and invited our ridicule, if he had? I am inclined to believe this extraordinary story.'

'You! With your passion for logic and precision! I doubt that!' Lestrade's tone was incredulous.

'Thank you, Mr Dorey, for your valuable assistance. One last question: you say that you did not mention this matter to anybody but Warburton. Do you happen to know whether or not the colonel spoke to anybody about it?'

'I believe that he told Major Merridew something of it.'

'But they are very close friends,' said Holmes carelessly. 'That is very natural. Well, thank you once more, and a good day to you!'

And with this cheery farewell, Holmes left the medium's house, with Lestrade and I wide-eyed behind him. Outside, his face was as inscrutable as ever.

'There is material here, gentlemen, there is scope. It seems to me to be a very dangerous man with whom we are dealing.'

'You evidently saw more in Mr Dorey's words than we did ourselves, Holmes,' said I.

He shook his head. 'No, Watson, but I fancy I deduced a little more. Well, Lestrade, what will you do now?'

The little official smiled a mocking smile. 'Go back to the station and test my deductions,' said he. 'I think it is only a matter of time before I have sufficient evidence to effect an arrest. It seems once again, Mr Sherlock Holmes, that you desire to chase off after trivialities and lose sight of the main objective. Well, chase all you like, but I've got a murderer to lay my hands on and I shan't do it standing here chatting. If you ask me, it's him in there who's to swing for it! So you go your way, and I shall go mine!'

Holmes chuckled softly. 'And if my trivialities bring any fresh developments, Lestrade, I shall find you at the station? Very well! Goodbye, and happy hunting! Watson,' he added, as Lestrade left us, 'how is your Biblical knowledge?'

'No better than the next man's.'

'Do you know what happened when Christ was crucified? No? Then I shall tell you. My own knowledge is not so rusty as it once was. The Roman practice of crucifixion adhered to very precise procedures. After sentence, the victim was flogged, thus weakened by loss of blood. His outstretched hands were then fastened — either by thongs or by nails — to a heavy wooden beam that was placed across his shoulders. This beam was affixed to a vertical one, and the victim was left hanging there — to die.

'Your medical knowledge will no doubt tell you that hanging thus from his hands would render it impossible for the victim to breathe, unless his feet were secured to the cross. If so, then he would be able to press down upon them and relieve the pressure upon his chest. In this way, he would live for a day or two more than if they were not fastened. Either way, my dear Watson, if the victim did not die satisfactorily quickly, his agony was terminated by breaking his legs. The Gospels indicate that Christ's tormentors were to do just that, before they were forestalled.'

Holmes had delivered his narrative with his piercing eyes fixed upon me in a most serious manner. My mind reeled, for I was dazed by the horror of the thing.

'You mean to say,' I gasped, 'that Warburton was *crucified*?'

'Consider the facts! The rope marks upon his wrists, indicating that he had been tied up; his legs, apparently unnecessarily broken; the asphyxiation. Miss Warburton said that her father had been missing for almost two days before his death was discovered. Where was he? He was hanging, dying, in a way that no man could have imagined still existed! You saw those hooks in the outhouse wall? Suppose he had been tied to them, or one similar to them, with outstretched arms and dangling legs. That would cause the great weight upon his chest, which would lead to asphyxiation, and death. A gag would prevent him from crying out for help.'

'And his face, too!'

'That would explain the expression on his face, which suggested that he had foreseen his own end. A slow death, Watson, one that he could feel encompassing him more and more each second. What more apt description of crucifixion than that?'

'It is horrible!'

'Now you see the implication of Dorey's visions? They were allegorical, not metaphorical! The danger was not from the church or from Craddock, but from a form of death associated with the church! Indeed, the very death of Christ Himself!'

'And then it is as you said?' I cried. 'The attacks upon the church door, the altar, and even upon the vicar, were attempts to defend himself against the church, for that is where Warburton believed the danger to lie!'

'Precisely, my dear Watson!' replied

Holmes. 'Warburton's madness was nothing more than fear of what he believed was his nemesis. Dorey had misinterpreted his vision, and drove the colonel into a wild frenzy!'

I stared at Holmes, in my eyes a mixture of horror and disbelief. I was revolted by the idea that such a terrible form of execution could still be contemplated in a civilized society. Had we not advanced over the past two thousand years from our ancestors? It was as though time's passing had meant nothing, and as if we had learned nothing from history's mistakes. That thought alone sickened me more than even the conception of this hideous crime.

'Who is this diabolical fiend in our midst?' I hissed.

'That is a matter of clarification, Watson,' said Sherlock Holmes. 'I have an idea, a suspicion, but nothing more.'

'What ideas?'

'If our supposition is correct, then Warburton's murderer must have had a place to conceal the dying man's body; a place where no one could simply stumble upon his victim and reveal the atrocity. And there lies the importance of Harvey's statement, which you missed entirely! You remember that he told us that all the houses hereabouts have outhouses, and all the outhouses have hooks similar to the ones in Warburton's own outhouse? That was a most significant clue. What better hiding place and torture chamber? Imagine! The devil hangs Warburton from the hooks, some twelve feet off the ground, and there he is suspended until he is dead. His legs are broken to quicken the process, and the lifeless body deposited in the woods.'

A thought had struck me. 'How did the murderer get Warburton into the crucifixion pose? Surely he would have struggled?'

'Certainly, but what if the murderer is someone whom the colonel knew well? Someone whom he trusted? If so, he would go willingly into the outhouse, suspecting nothing, and once inside, the killer has merely to overpower him. Remember that he is an old man whose constitution has been weakened. To overpower him would be no difficult task.'

'But what motive can there be?' I protested. 'And why choose such a terrible method?'

Holmes was silent for some time, his eyes fixed upon the darkening sky. A chill breeze had begun to blow, as though the elements were reflecting the horror of the Warburton business by sending similar chills through our bones. Finally, my companion turned to me and shook his head.

'As to the first question, I have no clue as yet, Watson,' said he. 'There must be a motive, and rest assured I shall find it. I believe that the answer to the second question will bring light upon the first, and when we find it we shall have our man firmly in our grasp. Now, however, I shall leave you, Watson, for there are one or two things that I should like to do alone. I shall meet you back at the vicarage in two hours, when I shall hopefully have an answer to all your questions.'

★　★　★

He did not return all the afternoon. It was late, about ten o'clock, when Craddock and I were sitting over a glass of brandy, and the maid came in with an envelope. It was addressed to me, and was from Holmes, asking me to meet him at the Chislehurst Arms immediately.

When I arrived, I found Sherlock Holmes sitting at a table in the corner. His eyes sparkled with triumph, and I observed that a half-emptied plate of wholesome food lay before him.

'You have eaten?' he said, as I joined him. 'Excellent food here, Watson, you should try it before we leave.'

'We are leaving?'

'Certainly. I can think of no reason to stay.'

'But the murderer!' I protested.

He laughed heartily. 'Oh! I have him in the palm of my hand! He does not know it yet, but I have, my dear Watson. Before this night is over, he shall be fluttering in our nets, as helpless as all the other unique exhibits in the Baker Street museum!'

Rising from the table, he beckoned me

to follow, and we made our way back to York Place. We reached the house, but Holmes continued walking, urging me to make haste. Finally, we reached our destination.

We had moved to the back of the houses, into the woodlands where the body had been discovered. We faced the back of the houses, so that to our right was the large and imposing silhouette of York Place, and in front of us a similar house, which I had never seen before. As Harvey had said, however, there was an outhouse similar to the one to our right, and it was to this that Holmes pointed. 'Our goal,' he whispered.

The house itself was in darkness, save for a single lamp burning in an upper window, which showed that the occupant — whoever it may be — had begun to retire for the night. Gripping me by the shoulder, to show that his actions were carried out after the deepest thought, Holmes began to scale the wall and hedgerow that bordered the garden of this mysterious domicile. When he reached the top, he cocked one leg over the wall, and sat astride it. With a signal for me to follow, he leaped with great agility to the lawn below. I joined him presently, my old wound giving me some trouble as I scaled the high brick wall, and he led me to the outhouse.

Putting his lips to my ear, he whispered softly, 'This is the key, Watson. I have been here once already, when the owner of the house was absent for some time, and I have seen the solution.'

Taking out an implement from his pocket, he picked the lock of the outhouse door, and gently pushed it open. He lit a match and we entered. The outhouse was small, and used to store various tools for cultivating the garden, and a faint odour of creosote was in evidence. Holmes turned to me, his aquiline face exaggerated by the flickering of his match.

'Look there!'

He moved the light to the very darkest corner of the storehouse, and I saw a thick coil of rope, tossed carelessly behind a wooden box. Lighting a fresh match, Holmes moved across to the dark recess and pulled the rope carefully into our view. Handing me the match, he took out his lens and closely examined the ends of the rope. Even without the glass, it was clear that the rope had been cut through.

'No doubt this was the rope used to secure the poor colonel to his crucifix.'

'Holmes!' I stammered. 'Look!'

Pointing across to the far wall, we saw, as Harvey had said, two hooks attached to the wall. They were similar in size to the ones we had seen earlier that day in Warburton's own outhouse, and yet there was one terrible difference. Attached to these hooks, there were two pieces of rope, which matched exactly the coil that Holmes held in his hands. This, then, was the torture chamber, the scene of Warburton's horrific death.

'What the devil are you doing here?'

The loud, booming voice had come from behind us, the door having been thrown wide. Turning around, I gasped, for the author of the question was known to me, and his identity shocked me beyond all measure.

'Well, well,' said Sherlock Holmes

cheerily, 'I thought you had retired to bed. It seems I was mistaken.'

'Yes! You were!'

'Do not be noisy, sir, or else you will wake the neighbours, and I am sure you would not wish them to know what a disgrace you are to your decorations, Major Merridew!'

The tall, thin soldier snarled viciously at my companion, and drew out a revolver from his pocket. I felt my hand reach instinctively towards my own pocket, and felt the butt of my own revolver inside.

'And I am sure that you would not wish to have your reputation tarnished,' hissed the major. 'The great Sherlock Holmes, nothing more than a common burglar!'

'It is a role I have assumed many times before, and with some considerable success.'

Holmes stepped coolly out of the storehouse and walked up the lawn. Then, turning to face Merridew, he said simply, with a hint of blandness in his voice, 'Why?'

Major Merridew stepped forward,

seemingly ignorant of my presence, but keeping my companion within his sight.

'He had to be done by as he did to others,' he snarled. 'He killed more men than I have ever harmed, Mr Sherlock Holmes, but the law was on his side. Such is the irony of a military life.

'Years ago, during the Indian Mutiny in fact, we were in the same regiment. He was in charge of a strategic ambush at Lucknow, as I am sure you are aware, and the success of the mission would have won us all the Victoria Cross. We set out, ready to attack, and armed to the teeth. Many of the lads there were young, hardly twenty-one, and I cared about them all. But I cared for one more than any other soldier on that battleground. He was my brother, Stanley, ten years my junior, but with more courage than a man twice his age.

'We reached the rebels' camp, and were ready to advance. Stanley and I were ready, side by side, intent on showing them what Hell was like. We waited for Warburton to give the order to move, our hearts in our throats and our stomachs in our boots, but ready to give our lives for the cause. And Warburton stood silent. He could not move, his brain rushing with thoughts about the merits and moral of our actions. That hesitation, that one moment of cowardice, was all the rebels needed. They saw us, and it was they who attacked us! I barely remember anything about it, for a heavy blow thundered across my spine and I was down straightaway. My world drowned in blood, but I felt strong arms around my shoulders, and felt myself being carried away to safety.

'In a matter of moments, most of our company lay dead, and barely a third remained standing.' His voice quickened, and the hand that held the gun shook with the emotion surging through his body. 'By a miracle, we were triumphant. Upon our return, Warburton was decorated for his heroism. But I knew what had happened, and to see that medal on his breast turned my soul to water. And among the forgotten dead, the true heroes of that campaign, there lay my dear Stanley, who had died trying to save the life of his brother. Is that justice? A hero gets nothing but an early grave, and the man who led us all to death gets rewarded with the prize that should have gone to my poor, brave Stanley.'

Holmes's eyes were like ice. 'But why did you kill him now? After all these years?'

'Murder was not at the front of my mind, Mr Holmes. I wanted that man to suffer, to think on what he had done, and on the lives he had wasted! If he died, he died, and it was no matter to me. But I wanted him to suffer at the hands of that which he held dear. Stanley's only love was the army, and he had died at its mercy. So, too, would this disgrace of a man, Warburton.

'I thought and thought about it over the years, but I could not conceive of a way to get him. It was only when this man Dorey arrived in the village that the path was opened up for me. Warburton had told me that this medium had warned the old fool, against the cross and the church, and he described the vision that the psychic had had to me. At last I saw my revenge! He placed all his faith and love in the church — how ironic it would be if it finally broke him. And so I settled on it. He would suffer in the very way his Saviour had suffered for his sins!'

Holmes stepped forward. 'And so you took him to the outhouse, turned on him, and tied him to the hooks, allowing him to die a slow and painful death?'

'Yes! And in the end he could take no more, and so I smashed his legs! I cannot describe the pleasure it gave me, seeing this pitiful spectacle before me. There he lay, sprawled across the floor: a coward in life, and a jest in death.

'But now, Mr Sherlock Holmes, you appear to know more than I can permit, and so it is time for you to throw off your mortal coil, as they say.' And raising the pistol, he aimed at my friend's head, as Holmes stood as solid as a rock before him.

I have said that the major had forgotten my presence, so wrapped up was he in his own egotistical world. And so it proved, for I was able to take out my pistol and place it to his head, warning him that I was willing to use it if necessary. Turning to face me, I saw the madness in his eyes for the first time, and it was a sight that saddened my very heart. To see a military man, as honoured as the one before me, sink to such depths of inhuman sadism and cruelty turned me sick. As he saw the futility of his position, he smiled, and then laughed a cold and mirthless laugh of unrepentant horror, as Holmes slowly took the revolver from his shaking hands.

★ ★ ★

'You see, Watson,' said Holmes, as we sat together in Baker Street the following morning, 'once I had defined the means of murder, everything fell into place.'

We had informed Lestrade the previous night of Merridew's guilt and of the steps that we had taken to unmask him, and he had been taken into custody for questioning. Holmes had surmised that his sentence would not be capital, due to his poor mental health, and the certainty that he would answer for his crimes at a higher court than the Assizes. We returned home, therefore, where Holmes gave me a brief account of his reasoning in this most grotesque of affairs.

'It was clear,' he continued, 'that Warburton was not mad but frightened, and that the cause of his fear was the church. As you said yourself, why destroy something that you once revered? To believe that he feared the church as a building was absurd, and so I began to surmise that he feared the church as a symbol. The presence of the medium, Dorey, was confirmation that the affair was content to cross the boundaries of the tangible and the intangible. The state of the body and the violence of the crime convinced me that a terrible means of murder had been employed, and it was Dorey's supposed vision that gave me the idea. He had dreamed of a crucifix, so why might that not be the method of murder?'

'But why give credence to Dorey's 'power'?'

'I didn't. To a mind like mine, Watson, such ideas are inadmissible. Even now I can see no evidence for Mr Dorey's claims. What mattered to me was that Warburton *believed* in the fanciful idea that a man could predict the future. Belief is a very powerful weapon, Watson, and often a dangerous one. So it proved here: Dorey was so adamant that he was gifted that he convinced Warburton of it also, thus forcing the colonel to believe it! Merridew merely manipulated this belief.'

'What led you to him?'

'When we first met, if you recall, I asked him whether the colonel could have died naturally, and he replied that the condition of the body would answer my question for me. And yet Lestrade informed me that Merridew had, in fact, not seen the body, and that only Harvey, the local constable and the inspector had done so. How, then, came Merridew to know the state of the corpse? Clearly, he had seen it at some time. My suspicions became certainties when I found the hooks in the outhouse, which would have served the purpose of the crucifixion. The matter seemed final when young Harvey told me that all the neighbouring houses had similar outhouses with identical hooks. What better place to hide a body, if he were a murderer?

'I became convinced of his guilt, and decided that a search of the outhouse would prove valuable. Once there, I found the rope tied to the hooks that corresponded with the marks on Warburton's wrists, and the coil from whence it had been cut. I brought you back with me so that I might have a witness to the confession I felt sure I would get. Merridew was a psychotic egomaniac, and there is no one more likely to talk about himself than such a gentleman.'

I sank back in my armchair with a sigh. 'It seems so simple now that you explain it. Will you wire to the Reverend Craddock and explain the situation to him?'

'I shall,' replied Holmes. 'I only hope that the gossips have not beaten me to it.'

He did so, and we received a letter from our client in return, thanking us for our assistance. Mr Craddock asked, however, that we did not make the facts of the case public. Elise Warburton had suffered enough, he said, and nothing could come of a publication whilst any member of the family was alive.

'There is some truth in his words,' said Holmes thoughtfully, as he put the letter aside. 'For the present, Watson, file it away in our archives, for it is a distasteful case, and one upon which I do not wish to dwell. Bury the case in your indices, Watson, and I shall file the name Merridew in my fine collection of M's, where I hope it shall remain only an abominable memory. Now, Doctor, if you would be so good as to touch the bell, I think some of Mrs Hudson's grouse would serve as an excellent prelude to a night of Covent Garden and Wagner.'

The Adventure of the Hollow Bank

It will be remembered by those members of the public who have taken such a keen interest in this series of memoirs of my friend, Sherlock Holmes, that I was at school with a lad by the name of Percy Phelps. I find it in my notebook that I have had reason to mention Phelps before, in the case of the theft of the Triple Alliance Treaty, and that in my account of that affair, I mentioned my childish antics of chivying him about the playground, and hitting him over the shin with a wicket. My counterpart in this somewhat unpleasant pastime was a boy called McGregor Abernetty, who, like Phelps, went on to rise in his chosen profession, and whose years of ill health brought Sherlock Holmes and me into one of the most remarkable but dreadful cases of our long association together.

It was, I remember, a blazing hot day in August when Abernetty's name was recalled to my memory after so many years. The Baker Street rooms seemed to be almost tropical in their temperature, and the glare of the houses opposite was so painful to the eye that I had found it necessary to draw the blinds. Holmes lay curled up on the settee, his head sunk into a cushion, and a dusty, leather-bound volume in his hands. For myself, I was occupied in a cursory glance through *The Times*. There was, however, little to interest either my companion or myself. There had been very few cases brought to his attention that could have satisfied both his analytical talent and that customary appreciation of the unusual, which was a feature of his capricious and artistic nature. There were numerous petty thefts, the brutal murder of a young barmaid in one of the seedier suburbs of the capital, and the kidnapping of a baby from Charing Cross Station; but none of these crimes appealed to Holmes's desire for the imaginative, and his love of the unusual.

It was into this situation that the letter from Abernetty was delivered. It arrived in the second post, and I read it several times and with increasing joy and amusement. It was in the peculiar, stiff hand that had been so prominent in our schooldays, and it ran as follows:

Hollow Bank
Wiltshire

My Dear Watson,

I have no doubt that my name has passed beyond your recollection, and that you will hardly understand the reason for this communication, but the older one gets the more one yearns for one's friends. It is unfortunate that an intelligent race such as ours should be so foolish as to allow its happiness to fade by losing touch with those people who gave us joy and with whom we spent such pleasant times. Indeed, I still remember with a smile the two of us persecuting young 'Tadpole' Phelps around the yard with a wicket, and getting into serious bother about it from Old Addy, the Classics master. It is memories like these that have prompted me to communicate with you, for I understand from my wife that you are now in a position of some note, being the friend and associate of a man whom I have grown to admire a great deal. I write, therefore, to invite you to Hollow Bank, in the hope that our shared memories will be as warming to you as they are to me. Please, bring Mr Holmes down with you, should he not be too busy. There is a train from Waterloo, I understand, and Jarvis can meet you at the station.

Your old schoolfellow,
MCGREGOR ABERNETTY

I showed the letter to Holmes, who read it with a look of uninterest on his face. 'I have never heard you speak of this man Abernetty,' said he.

'He had passed from my mind completely.'

'The man is an old campaigner like yourself, I observe,' said Holmes.

'He served in Afghanistan, although we

were not in the same regiment.'

'Indeed. The stiff handwriting is characteristic of the bearing of a military man. I perceive also that he is an inveterate taker of snuff, is particular in his habits, and that a strong streak of sentimentality runs through his veins. I note also that he has recently spent some time in China,' he added, tossing the letter across to me.

I stared in wonder at him. 'How can you possibly know all that about a man you have never met? You are exaggerating, surely?'

Holmes closed the leather volume, which was resting on his knee, and lit his cherrywood pipe. 'It is simplicity itself, my dear Watson. Observe, if you will, the way in which the letter has been folded. Had he used a measuring rule, he could not have folded it so perfectly in half. That indicates a man of particular habits, and this notion is further suggested by the complete absence of any inkblots and the fact that the writing is perfectly straight across the paper. Ordinarily, one would expect some fluctuation in a man's handwriting, but this is flawless. Clearly, your friend is a man of meticulous habits.'

'But the sentimentality?' I protested. 'It is true, I grant you, for we used to comment upon it at school.'

'What else can be indicated by the melodramatic phrases in the letter about yearning for old friends? A sensible, level-headed man like yourself may miss his old acquaintances, but to yearn for them suggests some measure of sentiment.'

'And the snuff?'

For answer, Sherlock Holmes handed me the envelope that had contained the letter. 'Observe the inside corner,' said he. 'You will find minute traces of snuff, which must have fallen into the envelope before he sealed it. Doubtless it would have caused him a great deal of annoyance had he noticed it. As to China, you have only to observe the Oriental design of the watermark on the paper to infer such a visit.'

I smiled at the ease with which Sherlock Holmes explained his reasoning, and at the careless shrug of his shoulders at the simplicity of his deductions. I re-read Abernetty's letter once more, and paid particular attention to his invitation to bring Holmes down to Wiltshire with me. I knew that it was not in his nature to take an aimless holiday, and that he disliked leaving his practice for any length of time. Work never tired him, but he was perpetually exhausted by idleness. Upon my asking him whether he would be willing to spare me a few days, however, I was surprised by his genial acceptance.

'Since the London populace has forfeited any hope of interesting crime, and the press being as stagnant as it is, I should be happy to accompany you. If your practice can accommodate your absence, I think the country air will do us both the power of good.'

There was, as Abernetty had said, a train from Waterloo and we caught this in good time. Jarvis, a small and pugnacious man, met us at the station and drove us in a brougham to Hollow Bank. Jarvis was the butler at the house, as his manner and dress made testament, and I understood that he had been in Abernetty's service for most of his life. As we climbed into the carriage, I saw that there was an air of sadness in his demeanour, and I could not help but notice that his eyes, which were dark and inscrutable in colour, were swollen, which suggested to me that he had recently been crying. Sherlock Holmes noticed it also, for I saw that his own keen eyes narrowed as the butler greeted us, but he said nothing to me upon the subject as we rattled on our way to Hollow Bank.

The house itself was magnificent. It had been built around the time of the Norman Conquest, as a plaque above the entrance declared, and it appeared to have remained unchanged throughout the centuries. There was, of course, some modernization to one or two of the wings, but the main structure of the building, the small windows and the heavy-lintelled door in particular, spoke only too clearly of their ancient history. A long line of evergreens lined the dusty drive leading to this entrance, and formed an impressive, almost regal, approach to the house. The fine park in which it stood gave the impression of such isolation, that for a moment I seemed to be separate from the bustle of the world in which I lived. The squabbles of Parliament, the squalor of the city and the tragedy of crime all seemed to be lost in those gardens and a sense of calm washed over me that I found difficult to dispel. Only the sadness that I saw so clearly in Jarvis's eyes reminded me of the troubles and uncertainties that plagued our society.

Standing in the doorway was a tall, aristocratic man with some considerable bearing, although his knees were beginning to bend. He wore a very fine, grey tweed suit, and a pipe thrust from his thin lips. An impressive moustache, the colour of the purest snow, adorned his face, and added to his already impressive visage an extra touch of the pride of his countrymen. His eyes were bright and looked out at us with anticipation and joy. The years had treated him badly, I observed, for although we were of the same age, he seemed to be ten years my senior. And yet as he stood there, McGregor Abernetty still managed to exude all the presence of power with which he had amazed us at school, and that had earned him such respect in the forces.

'Why, it is good to see you, Watson,' he boomed with that same authority in the voice that I recalled so well. 'You have changed very little, although I wonder about the moustache.'

'I am pleased to have been able to accept your invitation,' said I. 'It has been such a long time.'

He looked at me kindly, and there seemed to pass between us a sudden rush of memories. At last, his eyes passed over my shoulder and fell upon my companion. Sherlock Holmes had been standing some distance away from us, his keen eyes darting across the extensive lawns to which I have alluded. At my request, he came forward and McGregor Abernetty shook his hand warmly.

'It is a pleasure indeed to meet the foremost champion of law of our generation,' said he. 'My home is honoured.'

'Thank you,' said Holmes simply, although I could see that he was pleased by his host's remarks.

We were shown to our rooms, and having unpacked our cases, we joined Abernetty in the drawing room. He sat on a leather settee, with a glass of whisky in his hand, and upon our entrance he rose, rang the bell, and Jarvis arrived promptly. Holmes and I ordered a whisky each, and the butler departed. As he did so, I turned to Abernetty and jerked my thumb towards the door.

'Jarvis has been with you some time now,' said I.

'He has been the most faithful retainer a man could wish for. The house runs smoothly and in proper order thanks only to Jarvis's competence and ability. I owe him a great deal.'

Holmes, who was standing at the window, put his finger to his lips and gave a murmur of an inquisitive nature. At the sound, both Abernetty and I looked up at him, and he smiled genially.

'Forgive me,' said he, 'but my mind was wandering. I was considering Jarvis, and how happy he must be in his work. After all, one would not remain in the same place for so long were one not content.'

'Quite so,' said Abernetty. 'He is very happy indeed.'

'And yet,' said Holmes in a tone of voice that I knew so well, 'he has recently shed a good many tears. There are distinct signs around his eyes.'

Abernetty rose somewhat uneasily. 'I see you have chosen well in your own particular profession, Mr Holmes. You are, of course, correct. Last night, he received a piece of unhappy news. His daughter, whom I believe he has not seen for some years, has died.'

'A tragedy indeed,' I said. 'They were close?'

'As I say, Watson,' replied Abernetty, 'they had not spoken for some time. She used to work as a maid in this very house, and always showed the respect and politeness so evident in her father. But there was, I believe, a family disagreement and the girl left to work in some tavern in London. The exact details I do not know, and Jarvis refused to speak of it. Then there came word yesterday of her death. To lose a member of your family, even after a violent disagreement, is a terrible thing.'

We were silent for some moments, as Jarvis entered with our drinks. I turned to look at Holmes as the melancholy butler went about his duties in the room, and I saw those alert, grey eyes following the man around the room. Something had aroused his curiosity, I felt sure, but when Jarvis left, Holmes turned his back to us and stared once more out of the window. I looked back at Abernetty and for a second our eyes fixed upon each other, before we broke into simultaneous smiles and began to talk of happier times.

We reminisced about school for a good part of that sunny afternoon. I reminded Abernetty of some of the pranks we had got up to, which he had forgotten; and he, in turn, relived for me a great number of adventures that we had had during those long terms. Our conversation naturally progressed to Percy Phelps, and Abernetty listened with the utmost attention and interest as I recounted as best I could the singular affair of the Naval Treaty, which had brought Phelps and me back into contact. From there, my host developed a desire to know more about

Sherlock Holmes, who had by this time left us to our memories. I heard with some sadness that the years in the tropics had ruined Abernetty's health, and this accounted for his weak knees and his lined face. He assured me that he was fit enough within himself, but I could see that he had more than enough unease inside his mind. Nevertheless, it was a pleasant afternoon, and the time passed so quickly that before I had gathered myself, it was almost time for dinner.

At dinner, Sherlock Holmes and I were introduced to the household with whom we were sharing our accommodation. Abernetty's wife, Constance, I remembered hazily from the time of their marriage, but I had forgotten what a kind and gentle face she had, and how brightly her eyes shone. This brightness was reflected in their daughter, Louise, who was, it seemed to me, the very image of her mother as I remembered from those distant years.

Sitting across from Holmes and myself was Henry Abernetty, Louise's elder brother, and I find it difficult to convey the impression he made on me. He had arrived very soon after Holmes and I, having travelled from some business in London. Like his sister to their mother, Henry reflected his father's bearing, and he held his head high, his chin jutting forward like a heroic portrait, and his elegant nose displaying the pride that was so very obvious in his father. His hair was like a midnight sky, and although he wore it rather too long, it was undeniably luxuriant in its texture. His manner of dress was a little too gaudy for my tastes, but when I learned that he was an artist, this appeared to excuse itself. For all these qualities, however, I was filled with an uncontrollable sense of unease, and the young man's talk had with it a dangerous edge for which I could not account. I put it down to my own personal prejudices, for I knew from his father's own lips that the boy had always been a worry to his parents. He had been a wayward child at school, his artistic temperament and hot-headed ideas getting him severely reprimanded. I tried to dismiss these thoughts altogether when I looked across at Holmes and saw his own gaze was turned upon the young Abernetty, and his eyes were filled not with suspicion but with interest, and even amiability.

Our first few days in that hospitable house were uneventful when compared to the singular events that were to unfold. There was very little of any importance to capture the attention of my friend, and the only perplexing incident was in the middle of our first week, when the local bakery failed to provide Hollow Bank with its usual ration of fresh loaves. Our breakfasts, therefore, were to be incomplete, with the absence of any toast, but there seemed little cause for complaint about the issue. Indeed, Mrs Westlock, the cook, made provisions and we were treated to double rations each morning. This generosity was lost on Holmes, however, who preferred to spend his morning rambling around the gardens, and exploring the neighbouring woods.

It was the end of our first week, when a terrible shadow was cast over the house. The first Holmes and I knew of the matter was when we were seated on a small garden seat beside the huge pond in the centre of the grounds. This pond was a small wonder, sitting in the centre of the greenery like a miniature ocean of tranquil waters, and a legion of tiny forms of life darting through their environment. Holmes was philosophizing about the intricacies of the network of such a microscopic society, and its parallels with our own, when I interrupted him and pointed towards the house.

'Hello! Here is Abernetty,' said I. 'What can be the matter?'

'Our host seems to be in a state of some nervousness,' observed my companion.

It was true, for Abernetty was running towards us, as fast as his tired legs would carry him, and waving his long arms in a frantic effort to engage our attention. I rose and strode off to meet him. Finally, we were sitting together on that bench, and once he had caught his breath, my old friend began a very remarkable tale.

'It is the devil's work, Mr Sherlock Holmes,' said he, breathlessly. 'I can only thank providence that you are under my roof when this terrible business occurred, although indeed what I am to do I have no idea.'

Holmes held up a calming hand. 'Come, come, my dear sir,' said he. 'It must be a fault of the school you attended, for you share the bad habit of our friend Watson in telling a story wrong end foremost. Compose yourself, arrange your thoughts, and tell us quietly and slowly what has occurred.'

I took out my hip flask and handed it to Abernetty. He gulped a couple of mouthfuls and took from his inside pocket a small silver snuffbox. Helping himself to several large quantities of the substance, he settled himself on the bench and took a deep breath. At last, he seemed ready to speak, although I could still see in his eyes the signs of agitation that I have so often witnessed in others during my association with Sherlock Holmes.

'I must tell you everything from the start,' said Abernetty. 'I am the local JP in this district, and I have a good many calls upon my time. Every day there are letters pleading for my leniency, or else there are letters demanding that I make an example of some unfortunate boy who has got himself into a spot of bother. Well, sir, these letters take up much of my time, as I endeavour to reply to them all individually. Public relations go a long way these days, Mr Holmes, and a touch of the personal has never gone amiss. This morning, I rose early, and you had no doubt noticed that I was not present at breakfast. The reason for this absence was the fact that I had eaten already and was working hard in the study over this correspondence to which I have alluded. I was still poring over them up until ten minutes ago, when my occupation and my concentration were rudely interrupted.

'I had the study door open, and I saw my wife, Constance, pass the doorway. I shouted a greeting and she returned it, and said that she was going into the dining room to make sure everything had been cleared from breakfast. She is very particular about such details, Mr Holmes, and is the curse of the kitchen staff. No sooner had I heard the dining room door being opened, than a terrible scream assailed my ears. It was like a cry from the bowels of the earth, and I knew at once that it was Constance. I dropped my pen and rushed to the dining room.

'I saw my wife running out of the room, her hand clutching at her throat and tears running down her face. She wore an expression of the utmost horror, and upon my questioning her, she could do nothing but point with a shaking finger at the dining room door. By this time, Mrs Westlock had appeared, and I left my wife in her care, for I knew that she should not be left alone in such a state of shock. When they had gone, I turned towards the door.

'Watson here will tell you that I am by no means a nervous man, Mr Holmes, but I confess that my heart was thundering in my breast as I opened that door. I stepped into the room, and was at once struck by the sound of bird song, and the slight breeze that even now floats past our ears. I peered round the door, and saw at once that the window was open, and I thought that one of the servants had opened it, either at the request of one of my guests, or simply to air the room. I made a note to mention it to Jarvis, and for the first time it occurred to me that he had not appeared on the scene. Nobody in the house could have failed to hear my wife's cry, I assure you of that; why, then, had Jarvis not come to investigate? As I walked further into the room, I saw the answer to that question before me.'

McGregor Abernetty paused in his narrative, and his shoulders heaved with his excitement. I confess that in my own breast, the thrill of adventure had begun to stir, and I saw from the intense look of concentration upon the face of Sherlock Holmes that he was also greatly excited by his host's words.

'There, lying before me,' continued Abernetty at last, 'lay the butler. In his right hand he held a small butter knife, and his left was thrust out to the side, the fingers locked in a fist. His eyes stared up at the ceiling in a hideous, sightless glare, and his mouth was open wide, as though a scream had frozen on his lips. But these details I noticed later, Mr Holmes, for my attention was immediately gripped by the man's throat. It had been slashed from one ear to the other, and spilling out onto the dining room floor, there was — ' He put his hand to his own throat, as though in some psychological sympathy, and a choking sob cut short the sentence.

'The situation is perfectly clear,' said my companion. 'Tell me, when was this exactly?'

'Just ten minutes ago.'

'Was there any sign of anybody in the room?'

'None.'

'No dropped handkerchief, or cigarette end?'

'There was nothing.'

'How about the window? It was open, you say?'

'That is correct.'

'Were there any traces on the sill?'

Abernetty's brow creased in concentration, as he tried to recollect. 'I cannot be sure. I did not go too near the window.'

'That is unfortunate,' said Holmes in

that cold, unemotional manner that was characteristic of him. 'There may have been vital evidence there. What did you do, then?'

'I left the room and closed the door behind me. My nerves are, as I have told you, perfectly sound and I had recovered from the shock quickly enough. My mind turned towards you, Mr Holmes, and how fortunate it was that you were here at such a terrible time. I rushed out to find you and to place the matter in your hands.'

Holmes rose with a sudden burst of suppressed energy. 'You have not left the room unattended?'

Abernetty reached into his waistcoat pocket and produced a small key. 'I locked the door behind me.'

'And the window?'

'I did not touch it.'

'Now, I should be much obliged if you would direct me to the window. I should very much like to view the matter from the outside.'

We looked at him in some astonishment.

'You do not wish to view the . . . circumstances of the tragedy for yourself?' asked our host.

Sherlock Holmes waved his hand aside in a dismissive gesture. 'I have found myself very much enjoying your lawns, Mr Abernetty, and as I remarked to Watson the other day, this bracing country air does wonders for a fragile constitution such as mine. Doctor, you and our host make your way back to the dining room, and I shall meet you there presently.'

Guided by Abernetty's directions, Sherlock Holmes walked away from us, waving his stick in a merry farewell, and with the familiar spring that showed itself in his step when the prospect of a mystery and the revelation of some problem came before him. It was a peculiarity of my companion's nature that the tragedy and horror of crime was in some sense a blessing to him, and he was unable to see the distress it caused to others. It was this aspect of his character that earned him the reputation of being a reasoning machine and a brain without a heart. But to me, who knew his every mood and belief, it was clear that it was the exercise in logic, the opportunity of analysis and the execution of justice that appealed to him, rather than the crime itself. As he walked towards the dining room window on that glorious morning, I saw a man wrapped in the most perfect happiness, whose soul shone as bright as the summer sun above him.

Abernetty and I arrived in the dining room, with its hideous embellishment on the floor, and found Sherlock Holmes bending over the window sill. The window was still open, just as Abernetty had said, and the sound of melodious bird song drifted in through it. The beauty of the sound and the exemplary view of the garden afforded to us did little to dispel from our minds the ugly and horrific sight before us, however. The butler lay upon his back, his eyes staring wide, and his throat sliced open like any faceless carcass in a butcher's window. It took all my professional effort to prevent myself from reeling at the sight.

Sherlock Holmes held in his hands a

small magnifying lens, and was examining the sill with the utmost care. For myself, I plunged at once into a thorough examination of the body that lay before me. He had not been dead for very long, and from the state of the muscles, I determined that the terrible attack had occurred no more than a couple of hours previously. Glancing at my watch, and seeing that it was now close on noon, I estimated the time of death as being no earlier than half past ten. I said as much to Sherlock Holmes, but he appeared not to have heard me. Instead, his attention was fixed upon the latch of the window, and he was playing with the handle.

'This window opens from the outside as well as the inside, I observe,' said he.

'That is correct, Mr Holmes,' said our host. 'All the windows on this floor are so constructed.'

'That is really very singular. What do you make of it, Watson?'

'I see nothing very remarkable in that.'

'But surely it is very curious,' returned Sherlock Holmes. 'What is to prevent a common burglar from gaining access to the house without the need for a jemmy?'

McGregor Abernetty walked over to the window and pointed to a small lock on the window latch. 'These windows have latches that lock with the use of a key. To gain access through this window requires such a key. We are not so careless as you imagine, Mr Holmes.'

A thought had occurred to me that Abernetty's observation that the window had been open when he entered the room was now more complex than we had supposed. Might it not be that the window was opened to gain *access* to the room rather than to *depart* from it? I put my thoughts to Holmes, who nodded approvingly.

'Excellent, Watson, it was just the point I was about to make,' said he. 'But hello! What is this?'

His gaze was fixed over my shoulder, and turning around I saw before me the familiar trapping of any decent household sideboard, which ran along the far wall. Holmes climbed nimbly through the open window and walked over to the fine piece of oak furniture. There was a tray of condiments in the centre of it, a small carafe of water and a set of crystal glasses, and a large china butter dish, the lid of which had been removed. There was an alert light of interest in Holmes's keen and deep-set eyes, and for several minutes he stared at the items upon the sideboard.

Outside we heard voices, and the door flew open to reveal Henry Abernetty and his sister, Louise. The latter was in a state of extreme agitation, and held onto her brother's arm with a grip for which I would scarcely have given her credit. The young man approached his father, taking care not to allow his sister to see the terrible sight upon the floor.

'Mother is in a shocking state,' said he. 'We have just heard what has happened. Have the police been notified?'

McGregor Abernetty clapped his hand to his head. 'Good God! In all the confusion, and with Mr Holmes here, I have lost all my senses!'

Holmes walked forward with an authoritative stride, and spoke in those brisk, business-like tones that he so easily adopted.

160

'I suggest, Mr Abernetty, that you communicate at once with Scotland Yard. This is a matter of some brutality and the local force will not, I think, have the manpower to deal with it.'

Louise Abernetty clutched my companion's sleeve, her eyes swollen with emotion. 'What has happened, Mr Holmes? What evil has struck this house?'

Sherlock Holmes had a remarkable courtesy and gentleness in his dealings with women, and was able to put aside his mistrust of them when the circumstances dictated it. At this present moment, there was something in the simplicity of the girl's plea that seemed to touch him, for he took her hand in his own, and patted it warmly.

'It is a tragedy, of course,' said he; 'but nothing we can not put aright. Now, Mr Abernetty, here is the name of a trusted colleague of mine.' He handed my old friend a leaf from his pocket book. 'Contact that fellow at once and mention my name. He will come down with all speed.'

The old man ran off, and left us alone

with the young couple. Holmes turned at once to Henry Abernetty. 'This is a most important affair, Mr Abernetty,' said he, 'and one that must be solved at all costs.'

'I understand that, Mr Holmes,' said the young man with some little effort. 'We put ourselves in your hands.'

'In the first instance, when was the last time you saw Jarvis alive?'

Henry Abernetty ran his fingers through his luxuriant hair, and his brows knitted in thought. 'I saw him at breakfast, looking as dour as usual, poor fellow. And I saw him again at about a quarter past eleven.'

Holmes smiled broadly. 'Indeed! Where was he then?'

'In here. I was passing the window with my sister and I happened to look in. I saw him standing just where you are now.'

'Did you observe him also, Miss Abernetty?'

'I am afraid not,' said the girl. 'I was too busy admiring the beautiful sunshine, and telling Henry that he really ought to try painting the sunset tonight.'

The young man smiled. 'I ought to try

painting anything. I haven't picked up a brush in months.'

Louise Abernetty dabbed her eyes with her handkerchief. 'Of course, that was before we knew about . . . '

'Of course,' said Holmes thoughtfully. 'What was Jarvis doing in here, Mr Abernetty? Did you happen to observe that?'

'Not really. He had his back to me, but he was standing at the sideboard. I suppose he was just going about his business, preparing for lunch. Re-filling the carafe, putting out a new slab of butter, and polishing the silver, I should imagine.'

'Was the window open when you passed it?' asked Holmes.

'I believe it was.'

Sherlock Holmes fell silent, and his brows furrowed in the most intense concentration, and I knew that hundreds of thoughts and flashes of deductions were racing through his balanced but thoroughly amazing brain. Finally, he broke out of his reverie and smiled warmly at the young couple before him.

'Did you both enjoy your walk?' he asked.

Louise was the first to reply with a flush of colour returning to her pale cheeks. 'Oh! It was wonderful,' she said. 'I had just got to this side of the house when Henry caught up with me, huffing and puffing, poor lamb!'

She stroked his cheek fondly, and Henry blushed at the action. 'I am somewhat out of training,' he confessed.

Holmes clapped his hand upon his knees and walked towards the door. 'Well, I do not think I need to detain you any longer. Thank you, and rest assured that upon the arrival of my friend from Scotland Yard, we shall go some way to dispel this unpleasant mystery.'

They left us, and Holmes closed the door behind them. There was upon his face a languid and dreamy smile, but his eyes were alert with amused exultation, and it was evident that beneath the nonchalance there was some very great and repressed emotion. It was at such moments that he was fully in command of the situation, and I have learned from my years of association with Sherlock Holmes that it is folly to try to force him to speak, but rather to let him reveal what he may in his own time.

For the present, he walked casually around the room, circling it once, and then again, before turning to the body. This he gave the most cursory of examinations, and throughout it his eyes returned again and again to the sideboard. My curiosity got the better of me at last, however, and I tried to see for myself what it was that so concerned him. My search was in vain, however, for there seemed to me to be nothing unusual at all. The butter was a full slab, and the sprig of parsley that adorned the top of it had sunk some way towards the middle. The temperature was indeed hot, and the carafe of water that stood beside the dish looked as welcoming as an oasis in the largest of deserts. The silver was laid out to perfection, and there were plates stacked up in the furthest corner. There was nothing, however, which excited my curiosity the way it had my companion.

I turned back and found Holmes

standing at my side. There was that familiar glint of amusement in his eye, and a faint smile upon his thin lips. 'Does anything strike you as peculiar, Watson?'

I shook my head. 'It all seems most perplexing,' said I. 'I suppose some burglar made his way from the lawn into the house, and that the butler disturbed him whilst going about his duties.'

Holmes shook his head with some emphasis. 'That is unworthy of you, Watson, as I think you realize.'

'But the window was open.'

'We cannot be sure of that. It was open when Mrs Abernetty entered the room, certainly, but it may have been closed prior to that. Remember that the windows open from either side, and a key would enable a man to open them. The point is a simple one.'

'And the notion of an intruder?'

'Preposterous in the extreme. What manner of burglar is it that attempts his crime in broad daylight? Dismiss all thoughts along those lines from your mind.'

'What then strikes you about the affair?' I asked.

For answer, Sherlock Holmes turned upon his heel and moved to the door. He pulled it open, and framed in the doorway like an actor at centre-stage, he said, 'I simply draw your attention to the following points. Firstly, I ask you to consider the curious amount of toast consumed at breakfast; secondly, pray observe the depth that the parsley has sunk into the butter on this singularly hot day. Each point is suggestive in itself, but together they are certainly conclusive.'

I was fully aware of my companion's fondness for talking in conundrums, and I knew that the significance of his first point was that there had been no toast eaten at breakfast. It will be remembered that there had been some error on the bakery's delivery, which had meant that the house was without bread for a week. The full importance of this fact eluded me, however, and I could make no sense of the business about the parsley. It had, as Holmes observed, sunk a great deal into the butter, but I could read nothing from it, and with a shrug of my shoulders, I followed him out of the room.

I found him in the hallway in deep conversation with Miss Louise Abernetty. Holmes was speaking in a very intense manner, and the young lady was listening with all attention. As I approached, Holmes held out his hand in greeting. 'Good of you to join us, Watson,' said he. 'Miss Abernetty is to take us on a small walk around the grounds. I suspect we shall find it most instructive.'

We set off in the young lady's company. The lawns of Hollow Bank were, as I have said, splendid. There were ancient yew trees that had been cut into curious designs, and various shrubs and hedges scattered around, like small hamlets in the tapestry of the countryside. At the back of the house was a large sundial, and as we passed it I remembered for a moment the terrible fate of John Openshaw, which I believe I have had cause to mention elsewhere in this series of memoirs. We had reached the opposite side of the house to the dining room, when we saw a small hut, somewhat in need of repair, which Louise Abernetty told us was her brother's painting studio.

'He really is talented,' said she. 'But he neglects himself.'

'Does he spend much time there?' asked Holmes, pointing to the hut with his stick.

'He has not been there for many months,' came her reply.

'This is where you and your brother were walking this morning,' said he.

'Yes.'

'At about a quarter past eleven, I understand.'

'I remember Henry commenting on the time. He said it was rather early for Jarvis to be preparing for lunch.'

'Indeed. Where exactly did you meet your brother?'

Louise pointed in the direction whence we had come. 'I came from the front door and was walking around the back of the house, past Henry's studio, and in the direction of the dining room. I was just passing the sundial that you observed at back of the house when I heard Henry calling me.'

'He came from behind you?' asked Holmes.

'Yes.'

'That is very clear.'

A change had come over the young girl, and she turned her tearful eyes upon my companion's austere gaze. She held out a trembling hand, and her lips quivered with emotion. 'Oh, Mr Holmes, Mr Holmes!' she cried. 'You do not think poor Henry has anything to hide.'

'There is much to explain,' said Holmes blandly.

'But Henry was with me, Mr Holmes, right up until we saw you in the dining room. He never left my side.'

Holmes smiled gently. 'Then he has nothing to fear from me.'

'But all your questions! You seem to accuse him; I see it in your eyes!'

'In all truth, my dear Miss Abernetty, I accuse myself.'

'I do not follow you.'

'Of coming to conclusions too hastily. All will become clear, I have no doubt of that, and you have been of the greatest service to me. And now,' he added, lifting his hat courteously, 'I bid you farewell.'

We left her alone, and I confess that I

was loath to do so, for she seemed highly affected by my friend's interrogations. It occurred to me that she may need further comforting, but Holmes took my arm and led me away. We walked with some haste to the front gates of Hollow Bank, and Holmes wore an expression of the utmost seriousness. His brows were knitted, and his lips pursed in concentration. When we reached the gates, he held up a finger to me.

'There is an errand I would like you to run for me, Watson,' said he.

'I am here to be used.'

'Take a cab into the village and send an urgent wire to Mrs Hudson. Ask her to collect all copies of last week's newspapers up until our departure from Baker Street. She should not have thrown them away just yet. Then, catch the first available express to London, and retrieve these newspapers.'

'What am I to do then?'

'Then, Watson, you travel back of course.'

'But what is the object of my errand?' I persisted.

Holmes, however, gave a careless shake of his head. 'This is not the time for questions, Watson, but for action. Take yourself off, and when you return this evening, I hope to have the redoubtable Lestrade by my side. It was his name I gave to our host, and if the inspector has his wits about him, he will realize the urgency.'

★   ★   ★

I drove into the village and dispatched a telegram from a small but welcoming post office. Then I made my way to the station and caught the first available train to London. The journey was tedious and seemed to last an age, for my mind was back at Hollow Bank and the dark business that had shrouded that beautiful house. As I had done so many times before, I endeavoured to form a theory, after the fashion of my companion, which would fit the facts as we knew them. Henry Abernetty had seen the butler alive at quarter past eleven. Constance Abernetty had entered the dining room and discovered the body at twelve. The murder must have occurred between these times, therefore, and I myself had estimated the time of death at being between half past ten and midday. The crime, then, was certainly one of opportunity and seemed to me not to be premeditated. But by whom? Henry and his sister were together for the time in question, and Mrs Abernetty was surely incapable of such a terrible crime. She was too proud a lady to be considered.

My mind turned irresistibly to McGregor Abernetty, and I confess that I was unsettled by the dark thoughts that formed in my head. He had been alone in his study at the time of the murder, but there had been no one with him to verify the claim. Would it have been possible, I mused, for him to go to the dining room, commit the crime and return to his study before his wife passed the door? He was not a healthy man, but the dining room was next to the study. But how, then, came the window to be opened? My mind raced with thoughts and questions, until finally I banished further suspicions from my brain. McGregor Abernetty had been a close friend of mine for many years at school, and I found it impossible to believe him guilty of such a terrible crime. But in the back of my mind, I heard Holmes's voice stressing the necessity of an open mind as far as detection was concerned, and telling me not to allow personal prejudice to bias my judgement. It was, he always said, of the first importance.

I tried to think instead of Holmes, and of the points to which he had drawn my attention. I thought about our past experiences and tried in vain to find some similarity in events that could aid me in finding some glimmer of the truth. What was the importance of the butter dish, and why was the absence of bread so vital? I cudgelled my brain to find some possible solution, but the whole thing was a tissue of mysteries and improbabilities. In the end, my head was whirling and by the time I reached the front door of 221B Baker Street, I was more at sea than before.

Mrs Hudson was forthcoming with the

newspapers Holmes had requested, although neither of us saw what importance or relevance they might have to the matter in hand. I turned the papers over and read them thoroughly on the journey back to Wiltshire, but nothing could I see of any importance. When I arrived back at Hollow Bank, I found Sherlock Holmes in deep conversation with the familiar figure of Inspector Lestrade.

'Ah, Watson!' said Holmes as I approached them. 'I see your quest has been successful. As you see, Lestrade has been as good as his word, and travelled with all speed to our side.'

'A pleasure to see you again, Doctor,' said the sallow inspector. 'Mr Holmes has told me of this dreadful business, and I must say it beats me cold. Why any man should take such a risk to commit murder as this fellow seems to have done is beyond me.'

'I confess it puzzles me also,' said I.

Holmes had buried his head in the newspapers, but his ears were as attentive as ever. 'Murderers invariably take risks,

Lestrade. It is a necessary part of the crime.'

I could see from his face that he had not found what he wanted in the newspapers, for he wore a downcast expression. He tossed aside copy after copy and fell into a deep silence. Ignoring his didactic tone, the inspector stretched out his legs and fanned himself with his hat.

'This case is a snorter, Dr Watson, and no mistake,' said he. 'To tell the truth, I'm not sure why Mr Holmes has brought me down here. There seems to be very little I can do.'

'You have not formed a theory of your own?'

'If it had been at night, I would have said it was a burglar and no mistake. But no burglar goes around in the daylight, and especially on these fine summer days!'

'Holmes has dismissed the idea of an intruder.'

Lestrade nodded in agreement. 'Rightly so, it seems. As I understand it, the son and daughter were walking around the perimeter of the house, just at the time the murder was apparently being done.'

'Henry Abernetty saw the butler in the dining room.'

Our conversation was interrupted by a sudden laugh from Sherlock Holmes, who now held a newspaper before his face, and his eyes darted over the words before him. He smiled at us and said how satisfying it was to find that one's memory served one so well. With that, he turned his attention back to the newspaper, and I knew that he had at last found the clue for which he was searching. What that clue was, and how he had known it was there, was beyond me, however, and I shrugged my shoulders. Lestrade merely shook his head in disbelief, and resumed his line of thought.

'So how come neither the brother nor the sister saw the culprit make his escape?' he asked. 'If he didn't go across the lawns, he must have gone back into the house. I suppose there's no doubt the window was open all the time?'

'It would seem to be the case,' I replied. 'Henry Abernetty says it was when he passed with his sister.'

'So the villain may have got in through the window, but he certainly could not leave by it or else he would have been seen.'

'If he did not leave by the window,' I ventured, 'he must have gone out into the hallway. He could not stay in the dining room.'

'But then why was he not seen by Mrs Abernetty? And why did Mr Abernetty not hear some noise from the study? His door was open, so surely he would have heard something.'

I nodded at Lestrade's suggestion, and in the back of my mind there reared my earlier thought regarding McGregor Abernetty, and I felt the sensation of suspicion like a dragon's breath down my spine. I put my thoughts into words, and tried to make it clear from my voice that they did not convince me.

'McGregor Abernetty guilty himself, eh? It is possible,' said Lestrade eagerly. To my dismay, he seemed adamant about my conclusions. 'In fact, it may be quite probable! He has no alibi, and he's a fairly big man, so would be capable of some violence.'

'I cannot believe in his guilt,' I said weakly.

Lestrade wagged a finger at me like an officious tutor to his pupil. 'Don't be too quick to jump to conclusions, Dr Watson. He may be a friend of yours, but that's no guarantee of his innocence. But what did he do with his clothes? He must have got rid of them somehow before his wife saw him, for judging by the body, a sorry mess they would be in.'

There was a sudden cry from Sherlock Holmes, and the inspector and I turned to find the famous amateur staring ahead. His eyes were wide in disbelief, and his mouth open wide. Finally, his face creased into a smile and enlightenment shone in his eyes. Clutching the newspaper that had given him such joy moments ago, he rose and clapped Lestrade on the shoulder.

'You really are an excellent fellow, Lestrade,' said he. 'It is a pleasure to work with you at times, and your process of deduction is coming along splendidly.

Now, gentlemen, I think it is time for tea, and I fancy Mrs Westlock would be very glad of our company just now. Would you both be so kind as to ask her to bring tea to the drawing room, and order me a large plate of sandwiches? I shall join you presently.'

'Where are you going?' asked Lestrade and I together.

'I am going to put Lestrade's theory to the test. If he is correct, then in all probability we shall have our case completed by dusk.'

With another congratulatory shake of Lestrade's hand, Holmes left us in the glare of the afternoon sun, shading our eyes with the frowns of our confusion.

Mrs Westlock was a very large woman, with an oval, ruddy face and a welcoming manner about her. The recent darkness of Hollow Bank had taken its toll, however, and this geniality had been replaced by a sombre expression. We had carried out Holmes's orders to the letter, and within ten minutes she appeared in the drawing room carrying a large tray of sandwiches and tea. We settled her on the settee with much difficulty, for she was adamant that her position would not allow it, but upon learning Lestrade's official capacity, she relented.

It was some moments before Sherlock Holmes joined us, and when he did so I saw from the smile on his face and the spring in his step that his plans were falling into place. He had seen a light somewhere amid this tangled affair, and I was confident that the truth was within his grasp. And yet to me, the whole business remained confused and grotesque. He fell into an armchair, helped himself to a beef sandwich and a cup of tea and sat for some moments in silence. At last, he turned his attention to Mrs Westlock and assumed that air of gentleness to which I have so often alluded.

'Mrs Westlock, please understand that this tragedy that has befallen the house is soon to be lifted,' said he. 'But to achieve that, I must ask for your candid assistance.'

The housekeeper nodded slowly, as though the grief of the events weighed on her own head. 'I shall do anything I can, sir, if it will help to make amends for poor Mr Jarvis.'

'How well did you know him?'

'Oh very well, sir, if I may be so bold. He had been here longer than me, but he never treated me with anything but equal respect. Some butlers think they run the house, but Mr Jarvis, he always said that working together made the house run itself.'

'How long have you been at Hollow Bank yourself?'

'A good fifteen years, sir.'

'And you have never known Mr Jarvis be in any trouble in that time?' Holmes's eyes were alert, and he stared at Mrs Westlock as though trying to probe her thoughts.

'How do you mean, sir? Trouble?'

'Had Mr Abernetty ever had cause to chastise him, for instance, or be upset with him?'

Mrs Westlock was adamant in her denial. 'No, sir, there was never any reason for the master to complain about any of us.'

'I see,' said Holmes and he lapsed into silence for a moment.

Mrs Westlock regarded him carefully, and I fancy she was somewhat perturbed by his thick eyebrows and clouded expression. In the silence, Lestrade saw his chance to take the lead and wasted no time in doing so.

'Now, then, Mrs Westlock,' said he, 'let's have some bare facts from you. What were you doing when you heard of the incident this morning?'

'I was about my duties as usual, sir, when I heard the mistress scream.'

'Can you hear that in the kitchen?'

'I was not in the kitchen, sir. In fact I was in here, airing the room.'

'Did you happen to notice anybody in the garden?' I asked, and was pleased to hear a murmur of approval from my companion.

'No, sir. As soon as I heard the scream I rushed out into the hall, and found Mrs Abernetty and her husband in each other's arms. She was terribly upset, poor dear.'

'You didn't notice any noise prior to

the scream?' said Lestrade with some eagerness.

'Not that I remember.'

Lestrade's tone began to show signs of impatience. 'There was no door opening or closing? Perhaps the study door?'

'I am sure there was not,' replied the lady with dignity.

'And then you took Mrs Abernetty away to calm her nerves?' said the inspector.

'Yes, sir. And some calming they took too. She drank more brandy than my man ever touched in his life.'

Sherlock Holmes rose suddenly, and helped Mrs Westlock to her feet. 'Well, thank you, Mrs Westlock, you have been of the utmost assistance to us. Oh, there is just one more question,' he added as she opened the door. 'Do you recollect Mr Jarvis's daughter, who used to work here?'

'Oh, dear Eliza, yes, sir. She was such an angel.'

'There was an upset, I believe.'

Mrs Westlock's face clouded. 'Indeed there was, sir, although Mr Jarvis never spoke of it.'

'Nevertheless,' said my friend blandly, 'I have spoken with enough servants to know that the scullery knows no secrets.'

She blushed uncontrollably. 'I am no gossip, sir,' said she. And then, after the briefest of pauses, she resumed. 'But it was the general thinking that poor Eliza had got herself into a spot of trouble. Hilary, the maid, thinks it was Bob Chapman, the grocer's boy, but Eliza would never have looked at an adolescent like that. She took a fancy to gentlemen.'

'But these were merely rumours, surely?' said Holmes, and I noticed that his thin fingers had become restless.

'Yes, sir,' replied the housekeeper, although her tone betrayed only too clearly her own faith in her words.

Sherlock Holmes clapped his hands together and rubbed them vigorously. There was a gleam in his eyes and a suppressed excitement in his manner, which convinced me, used as I was to his ways, that the truth was finally within his hands. My suspicions were confirmed when he suddenly burst into one of his rare fits of laughter. I have seldom heard him laugh, and it has always meant an evil time was coming to those whom he had set himself to hunt down.

'At last, we have the final link in the chain,' said he. 'Mrs Westlock is really the most excellent witness.'

Lestrade sighed with some contempt. 'I cannot see anything useful in what she told us.'

'Nor will you if you approach the evidence with preconceived ideas about a man's guilt,' replied Holmes sternly. 'It is inconceivable that McGregor Abernetty should be assumed guilty of a crime of which he knew nothing!'

'But he has no alibi — !' began Lestrade, but Holmes held up an authoritative hand.

'The true culprit has no alibi worth a candle either, Lestrade. And now, if it is all the same to you, I should like to take a short walk around the grounds before dinner.'

We followed him out of the drawing room and into the hall. Something caught my eye as I stepped into the passageway, and looking up I saw young Henry

Abernetty coming down the stairs. He hailed us as he did so, and Sherlock Holmes paced over to meet him at the foot of the stairs.

'Well, Mr Holmes,' said the artist. 'How fares the investigation?'

'There are one or two small facts upon which I need to be satisfied,' said Holmes, 'but all in all things are a little clearer.'

'May I ask if your suspicions point in any particular direction?'

'Oh yes.'

I stared in wonder at Holmes for a moment, for it was unlike him to be so candid about the results of his investigations. Even I, who knew him better than anyone, was not privy to his innermost thoughts until such time as he thought it necessary to impart any information, and even then it was only so much as he deemed discreet. And yet here he was, calmly revealing his deductions to a stranger, whilst insisting on leaving Lestrade and me in the dark. I had begun to protest, but my eye caught Holmes's and I read there that my silence would be appreciated, and he gave me a reassuring squeeze on my arm to show that all was within his control.

'I don't suppose you are at liberty to say any more,' Henry said at last.

'Certainly not, for any more information may prove dangerous for you to know, Mr Abernetty.' He leaned forward in a conspiratorial way. 'However, I can tell you that there has been a severe mistake on our man's part. He has left a vital piece of evidence in the place where he dumped it after the murder, and must be cursing himself about it now.'

'You are certain of this?'

'Of course, sir, I have seen it. I have not yet told my friend, the inspector, but first thing in the morning he shall seize it.'

Henry Abernetty clapped my friend on the shoulder and smiled. 'You are a marvellous man, Mr Sherlock Holmes. Let's hope this man you are after does not get to this evidence before you do!'

He walked away, still laughing, and disappeared into his father's study. Sherlock Holmes smiled after him, placed his hat upon his head and announced his intention of going for a walk. He would meet us back at the house for dinner, he said, and no more would he divulge about the matter in hand. He turned upon his heel and made for the door, twirling his stick, and whistling a jaunty but unrecognizable tune to himself as he went.

Dinner was a splendid affair, and was enlivened by Sherlock Holmes's conversation. Holmes was able to talk exceedingly well when he chose, and that night he did so choose. I have never seen him talk so well about all sorts of topics from miracle plays to Buddhism, each one handled with the brilliance of an expert. There was about my companion an air of distinction, and during the whole meal no one mentioned the dark business that had so blighted the past day. Even McGregor Abernetty, who had borne the strain upon his own shoulders, smiled at Holmes's gaiety and seemed to lose some of the deep-set lines in his face. Once again, sitting before me, I saw the fresh-faced youth with whom I had played at school, and there came into my mind the thoughts of suspicion that I had been foolish enough to conceive. How ridiculous they seemed now, sitting at that table in the same room where this horrible crime had occurred, when his proud face shone with the light of a thousand suns.

We ate well, and as the meal concluded, McGregor Abernetty thanked my companion for his wonderful discourse. 'It is a pleasure to meet a man of such diverse interests, and with such a grasp of a good many topics. You must read a good deal, Mr Holmes.'

'I have an infinite capacity for storing facts,' said Holmes.

'You are certainly a lively guest. Now then, I propose that we finish the evening with a brandy and a game of bridge in the drawing room.'

'Thank you,' said Holmes. 'Dr Watson and I shall join you presently, but my friend Lestrade will accompany you.'

The company rose, with the exception of Holmes and myself, and made its way to the drawing room. The door closed upon us, and I turned to my friend in amazement.

'Holmes!' I cried. 'What is the meaning of this? Where have you been all afternoon?'

He put a finger to his lips. 'Do not allow your voice to carry, my dear Watson. I have been collecting vital evidence that will throw some light on this dreadful business on the Abernetty family. It is essential that Lestrade is not present, or else our suspect will not come back.'

'Who?'

'The man who has brought disgrace on himself. If he suspects Lestrade is with us he will clam up like an oyster. But if we are alone, then the truth must come out. Hark!'

We heard the snap of the dining room door handle being turned, and the door creaked slowly open. Standing in the frame, silhouetted by the lamps that burned behind him, there stood a tall and patrician figure. I thought at first that it was McGregor Abernetty, for the poise of the head was the same, but upon hearing the voice I realized the truth.

'Where is it?' he said.

Holmes waved to an empty chair and lifted the decanter of wine. 'Pray sit down and take a drop of wine with us,' said he. 'It is always a pleasure to do business over a fine vintage such as this.'

'What have you done with it?' The voice grew more impatient, and the figure stepped forward into the light.

Seeing the features seemed to affect me more than merely hearing the voice, and when I saw that cruel mouth and the luxuriant hair falling in front of the dark, malicious eyes, I felt my heart tremble within my breast and my hands tighten upon my knees. I would have given my soul to have had my revolver in my pocket. Those dark eyes were fixed upon Holmes, and a thin, reptilian tongue passed over the dry, thin lips.

'The artist's smock to which you refer,' said Holmes, 'is in my bedroom. I removed it this afternoon after coaxing you into believing that the police would take it away tomorrow. I knew that you would make some effort to retrieve it, and that finding it gone would tell you that I was onto your little game.'

'Give it to me,' he hissed with venom, 'or else I'll serve you as I served Jarvis.'

Sherlock Holmes lowered the wine glass that he held in his hand, and stared over the candelabra at his prey. When he spoke, his voice was firm and showed no signs of any of the nervousness that leaped in my own heart.

'I have been threatened by better, wiser and far more dangerous men than you, Mr Henry Abernetty, and yet here I sit with you in the palm of my hand. Do not try to browbeat me for it will serve you nothing but ill.'

A change came over the young man at Holmes's words. He pulled back a chair and fell onto it rather than sitting down. There were beads of sweat on his lips and temples, and his hands clutched at the air nervously, as though trying to grasp some hope from the very environment around him. Holmes sat motionless, his eyes half closed, and his fingers drumming heavily on the table. 'What have you to say for yourself, Mr Abernetty?' said he.

'It had to be done. I could not allow father to know about . . . '

'About Eliza,' said Holmes, and at the name a spark of recognition flashed through my brain.

'Father is a tyrant in his own way. Any such scandal would have been unforgivable and I would be his son no longer. I have been in scrapes in the past — and I ask you what child has not? But there has never been anything like the trouble I got into with Eliza. It would have ruined me.'

'You would lose your inheritance,' said Holmes.

'Faster than a bolt of lightning in a darkened sky, Mr Holmes, and I need that money desperately.'

'What happened on that fateful morning, Mr Abernetty? Tell me the truth now, for I know as much of it as you do yourself.'

The young man buried his head in his hands, and spoke in between muffled, choking sobs. 'Jarvis and Eliza were close, closer than I will ever be to father, and they had no secrets. When Eliza and I became lovers, it was only a matter of time before she told him. Upon hearing it, however, Jarvis lost control of his senses. He said that it would mean the end of his position if my father ever discovered the truth, and that whilst he would support Eliza as much as he could, she must leave her place at once. There were a lot of tears shed, Mr Holmes, and I assure you that my heart dwindled with each one, for I knew that it was I who had caused them. I do not suppose that is easy for you to believe, but it is the truth.

'I continued to see Eliza in London, but soon realized that my finances were not up to it, and so I threw her over. I thought that the whole matter would end there, but a week ago I received a telegram from her saying that she was with child, and that there was no possibility of a mistake as to the father's identity. My world fell apart. What was I to do? I was not able to support a wife and child, and I could expect no help from my father.'

'Had Jarvis received a similar telegram?'

'Yes. He came and gave me hell for it. I was at my wits' end, Mr Holmes, and took the only way out I could think.'

'The telegram that Jarvis received to say that his daughter had died was, in actual fact, to say that she had been murdered.' There was no pity in Holmes's voice, and his cold eyes glared with distaste.

'Yes. When he found out Jarvis said he knew it was I, and that he would report me at once. But he would not go to the police, Mr Holmes, for he said that it was not his place to do so. Instead, he would tell my father. In either event, I was faced with ruin.'

Holmes rose and paced the room. 'So, you went to your artist's den and put on the smock that you wear when you paint, grabbing a knife from your palette. You ran over the lawn to the dining room window, let yourself in with your key, and murdered Jarvis where he stood. Then, exiting the way you had come, you deposited the smock and the knife back in the hut, and ran around to the opposite side of the house in time to meet your sister.'

'I thought that any medical evidence would show that he died between a certain time. The margin I had left for myself was, I thought, too narrow to be of any danger to me.'

'So it was. But you had not accounted for a piece of very vital evidence.'

'What was it? What gave me away, Mr Holmes?'

Sherlock Holmes opened the dining room door and called for Lestrade. As we heard the footsteps of the little official, my friend turned back to the wretched youth and said with more pride than I have ever heard in his voice.

'The evidence of the depth which the parsley had sunk into the butter.'

*   *   *

It was whilst we were sitting in the dogcart, *en route* for the station, that Sherlock Holmes finally filled in the answers to those questions that still haunted my mind. We had left the tragic house of Hollow Bank behind us, but the dreadful events of the past few days had not erased themselves from our memories, and still burned as brightly as a crackling fire. Holmes had allowed me to break the news to Abernetty of his son's culpability, and the old man had taken it better than I imagined. I knew, as he held his arms around me in farewell, that his pride would not allow him to show me any emotion, but that the sentimentality that so afflicted him would finally better him when we had left. Lestrade had remained behind, and Holmes and I rattled away from that terrible house.

'The point about the parsley in the butter,' said he at last, 'is a fine example of my belief that there is nothing so important as trifles.'

'Even now I confess to being in the dark as to its relevance.'

'The sideboard upon which the butter dish stood was not in direct sunlight, and yet the butter had melted so much that the parsley had almost disappeared into it. Henry Abernetty told us that, at quarter past eleven, he had seen Jarvis replacing the butter for lunch. Now, if the butter had been in the sun, then it would have melted a good deal in those forty-five minutes before the body was discovered. However, it was not in direct sunlight. How then could fresh butter have melted so quickly? And why had Jarvis replaced the butter at all, when none had been used at breakfast, due to the shortage of bread? The answer is, of course, obvious. The butter was not fresh at eleven fifteen, but had been standing on the sideboard since early that morning. Thus, it had melted and allowed the parsley to sink into it. That point alone told me that Henry Abernetty was lying about seeing the butler alive.

'But why should he lie about it? Clearly, his reasons were not honourable, and when I learned that he had been with his sister since that time the matter became clear. He wanted us to believe that the murder had been committed between eleven fifteen and midday, at a time when he was never out of his sister's sight, and therefore unable to commit the crime. I do not like being told what to think, Watson, and I was convinced that a false alibi had been clumsily concocted. In that case, the murder had occurred before quarter past eleven.

'At the same time, I suddenly remembered what Louise Abernetty had said about her brother. She had observed that he had been out of breath, as though he had been running. Now why should a man go running around the gardens of his house in such weather as this? The heat is almost unbearable when one is still, and physical exertion is surely folly in such temperatures. There had to be a reason for him to be so energetic, and that reason was becoming clearer.'

'Of course,' said I. 'The point about the windows being accessible from either side with the use of a key would seem to implicate a member of the family.'

'Precisely. The point struck me at once. Having satisfied myself that Henry was guilty, I set about proving it. The mention of Jarvis's dead daughter, who had gone to work in a tavern in London, recalled to my mind a story you read to me in *The Times* about a murdered barmaid in London. It was, I confess, a long shot, but upon receiving a copy of the newspaper from Mrs Hudson, I was less than surprised to find that the murdered girl had been identified as a certain Elizabeth Jarvis. For a daughter to be murdered in the same week as her father struck me as too much of a coincidence and I was satisfied that I held in my hands a motive for the murder.'

'I said myself that Henry was a wayward lad.'

'Indeed, and you were right. It is always useful to have a viewpoint of a person's character from one whose opinions you trust. In this case, I was willing to accept beyond doubt that Henry was a desperate man, who was not averse to taking risks.'

'What about the artist's smock?'

Holmes smiled at the question. 'The point was a simple one, but it is to my discredit that I owe its discovery to Lestrade. He will never know it, but without him I should have never been able to find any definite evidence against Henry Abernetty.

'Do you remember when Lestrade made the comment that the murderer's clothes must have been stained with blood? I had overlooked the point entirely. How could one man slit the throat of another and manage to prevent his clothes from being stained with blood? For an instant, I was at a loss to explain it, but when I recalled Henry's hobby, I saw the truth.

'He was a painter, and it is common for such artists to cover their clothes with a smock to prevent paint from splashing onto them. Such a garment would be ideal for our man's deadly purpose. Should anybody see him crossing the lawn wearing it, he can merely put it down to starting his hobby again, and no foul play would be suspected. The stains of paint already evident on it would conceal the bloodstains that would soon be spattered across it. The blood would be almost invisible. At a glance, who is able to differentiate blood and paint?

'It was this item of clothing that sealed his fate. The artist's hut was in a direct line to the dining room window, and was his obvious escape route. The time he took to reach his sister showed that he must have discarded the smock there, for he would have no time to do so elsewhere. There was every chance that he had not moved it since, and I placed all my hopes on it still being there.

'As you observed, I coaxed him into retrieving it, and then removed it myself when I left you and Lestrade. I knew that when Henry went to fetch it, he would see that there was someone very cunning upon his track. I dare say that dinner was excruciating for him, and I must confess to feeling a small quiver of pleasure at the thought. It was a distasteful, opportunistic crime, and one that could have been prevented had the young man had courage enough to ask his father for help.'

I nodded. 'Had he done so,' I said, 'I am sure that McGregor Abernetty would have taken pity on him. He is a proud man, but not a heartless one.'

'I am in agreement with you, Watson. And yet, it is easy to be wise in hindsight, and not so easy when one is in the thick of an emotional crisis.'

We had reached the station by this time, and were waiting on the platform for our train. As we stood there, I breathed the clean air of the country into my lungs, and looked with pleasure at the rolling hills of the deepest green merging with the light blue sky and the small, fleecy clouds scattered around it. The sun was bright in the heavens and yet there was an exhilarating nip in the air. I was a lover of the countryside and the sight of nature's own artwork filled me with pleasure, so used was I to the fogs of Baker Street. I said as much to Sherlock Holmes, but he merely shrugged his shoulders and shook his head.

'I shall be glad to be back in Baker Street once more,' said he with some relief.

'Why so?'

'The country fills me with a certain horror. I have remarked before, Watson, that when I look at these hills and fields, with the scattered farm houses and isolated cottages, I see only the impunity with which crime may be committed there. It is still my belief, Watson, and one which is based upon our most recent experiences, that the lowest and vilest alleys in London do not offer a more dreadful record of sin than this rolling and beautiful countryside.'

We do hope that you have enjoyed reading this large print book.

Did you know that all of our titles are available for purchase?

We publish a wide range of high quality large print books including:
Romances, Mysteries, Classics
General Fiction
Non Fiction and Westerns

Special interest titles available in large print are:
The Little Oxford Dictionary
Music Book, Song Book
Hymn Book, Service Book

Also available from us courtesy of Oxford University Press:
Young Readers' Dictionary
(large print edition)
Young Readers' Thesaurus
(large print edition)

For further information or a free brochure, please contact us at:
Ulverscroft Large Print Books Ltd.,
The Green, Bradgate Road, Anstey,
Leicester, LE7 7FU, England.
Tel: (00 44) **0116 236 4325**
Fax: (00 44) **0116 234 0205**

Other titles in the
Linford Mystery Library:

SHERLOCK HOLMES AND THE DISAPPEARING PRINCE

Edmund Hastie

The Crown Prince of Japan disappears without trace from his Oxbridge college rooms. Relatives of an heiress meet, one by one, with suspicious and grisly deaths. The thief of confidential battleship plans must be identified and located before the documents are leaked to the German military. And what nefarious activity links a cabman charging extortionate fares with a musically-minded butler? Narrated with wry affection by the long-suffering Dr Watson, each problem in this collection of four short stories showcases Holmes' well-honed skills of ingenious analysis and consequential deduction to perfection . . .

CLIMATE INCORPORATED

John Russell Fearn

When meteorologist Alvin Brook invents a means of controlling the weather, he imagines it will lead to his becoming a world benefactor, with riches for him and his family. Instead, Brook and his wife are murdered, and his invention is stolen and misused by industrialist Marcus Denham. Denham creates the mighty empire of Climate Incorporated, controlling the world's weather and holding nations to ransom . . . but he does not anticipate that outraged Nature — and Brook's son — will take their revenge.

DR. MORELLE AT MIDNIGHT

Ernest Dudley

Ian Laking is pathologically jealous of his beautiful wife, and obsessed with murder. His only hope lies in treatment by Dr. Morelle, the psychiatrist and criminologist. However Laking, suspecting his business associate Dyke Fenton of being his wife's lover, is plotting revenge . . . Dr. Morelle and his secretary, Miss Frayle, become caught up in the drama of jealousy and revenge. When the plan fatally recoils upon Laking himself, will Dr. Morelle be able to unmask the murderer?